Changeling Press, LLC

ChangelingPress.com

**Taken by the Satyr/
Taken by the Valkyrie Duet**
Paranormal Women's Fiction
Megan Slayer

Taken by the Satyr/Taken by the Valkyrie Duet
Paranormal Women's Fiction
Megan Slayer

All rights reserved.
Copyright ©2024 Megan Slayer

ISBN: 978-1-60521-928-8

Publisher:
Changeling Press LLC
315 N. Centre St.
Martinsburg, WV 25404
ChangelingPress.com

Printed in the U.S.A.

Editor: Jean Cooper
Cover Artist: Bryan Keller

The individual stories in this anthology have been previously released in E-Book format.

Table of Contents

Taken by the Satyr (Taken 5)
A Paranormal Women's Fiction Novel
Megan Slayer

Preston, son of Hermes, has a secret. He's been cursed to live as a satyr -- a monster with a dubious job he hates. He knows love is not in his future. Can't be.

Then he meets Lulu -- the daughter of a witch and Elf. A woman unsure of her place in the world. Luna has come back to Eerie to hide and heal, but a chance meeting with sorcerers and being thrown together with Preston changes everything. Love may be possible if only Luna can open her heart and change Preston's mind.

Chapter One

Back to the old homestead. Lulu snorted and pulled onto the dirt road leading to the witch enclave. She wasn't a witch herself. Hell, she wasn't even sure what she was -- the daughter of a witch and an elf. Did that make her a Wilf? An Elch? She had magic, but she wasn't good with spells. She couldn't bake for shit and refused to live in a tree.

She drove down the mucky path passing for a street to the house she'd grown up in. When she'd left for college, she'd been so wide-eyed and excited. So ready to embrace the world.

Then Tom happened. He'd consumed her life. He made her feel things. Showed her there was more to life, but most of it wasn't good. He needed control.

Of course, he did.

Being a sorcerer, he lived for control.

Every time she looked back on her last few years, she winced. She'd been so naive. She'd let him do all the things he'd done because she thought she loved him.

He'd never loved her.

But that didn't matter now. She'd broken free from his control, and he'd moved on to his next victim.

She stopped in her parents' driveway, but her thoughts clogged her mind. She'd considered his next girlfriend a victim. God. What a piece of work Tom was!

That didn't matter. She'd come home. She'd gone back to what she knew so she could heal her heart.

She left the car and strode over to the barn. Poofs of colored smoke shot from the chimney. Her mother must be creating.

She spied the plants in the field. Her father had

finally got the crops out on time. Good for him. A smile pulled at her lips. At least someone had their life going in the right direction.

She'd figure hers out soon enough.

She diverted from the barn and made her way over to the field. She breathed in the clean scent of the crops. Eerie was a hot mess at times, but it was also the place for paranormals to be themselves. It was a safe place.

She'd thought she needed a place to run away to, but not when home called. It wasn't like she had a lost love back home. She'd never had a boyfriend when she'd been in Eerie. She hadn't been enough of a paranormal -- not looking like an elf or witch. She'd been too normal, and teased for her appearance. Being different hadn't bothered her, though. She shook her head. She'd pulled herself up and grown. She wasn't the same girl who'd left town.

"You made it." Daff, her father, bounded up to her. "Got a lot to move in?"

"I'm not moving in, Daddy." She'd found an apartment on March Avenue, above a bakery. Sue her for liking the smells.

"I didn't think you would be, but I cleaned up the second floor just in case." He wiped his hands on a towel hanging from his pocket. "What are you planning to do?"

"I'm living in the Towers. Fourth floor. I'll get the keys this evening. It's furnished so I don't have to move anything but my clothes." She'd worked out a deal with Marina, her second cousin, to get the last furnished unit.

"Good. I'm glad." Her father hesitated. "Are you having a roommate?"

"No."

"Are you sure? A witch alone?" Her father shook his head. "We have room."

"You do, but I need to do this on my own." She hugged him. "But I appreciate the concern. I'm only a call away."

"I know," her father said. "Got a job yet?"

"At Linc's." She wasn't sure working at a restaurant and bar was smart, but it was a job.

"The bar?"

"In the restaurant. I head there next." She stepped back. "Just wanted to see you and Mom. I can use all the anchors I can get." She needed them.

"You're always welcome here."

"I know. Is Mom around?" She hadn't seen her, and her mother tended to be the center of attention.

"She's mixing spells with Grinella."

She should've guessed. "She spends a lot of time there with her."

"She does."

Sadness tinged his voice and she hesitated. "To the exclusion of you?"

"A bit."

"Daddy." She wasn't sure what to do to help him.

"She needs to find herself, so I'm letting her."

"But you're unhappy." She would be, too.

"I am, but I'll be here for her."

"What do you want? For you? Not for Mom?"

He stared at her. "I never thought about it."

"I know." She sat beside him on the fence. "What do you want?"

"To farm. To have my animals and work the land. To feel the earth in my hands. To be loved," he said. "All those things."

"Then that's what you should do. All of those

things. Have you told Mom you don't feel loved?"

"She's never home and when she is, she's drifting. It's like I can't reach her."

"You need to try and tell her." She hugged him. "I didn't tell Reuben how I felt, and it made life miserable. It would've changed so much and might have kept me from dating Tom." Might have made her life better.

"I will."

"You need to." She sighed. "I'll check on you, but I need to get to work."

"Go ahead. I'll be okay." He nodded. "It'll always be okay."

"You're sure?"

"I am." He offered a sad smile. "Go. Get your life going."

"I will." She hesitated before heading to her car. She wanted to be there for her dad. To help him have the best. For both him and her mother. She loved them and they did love each other, but they weren't good at communicating. Right now, they seemed pulled apart. Sort of like her situation with Reuben. He'd felt abandoned and used that feeling to walk away. He claimed he had to find his happiness. He hadn't cared that she was confused by her own feelings and overwhelmed. He didn't care that she wasn't sure how to deal with stress, but he wanted what he wanted when he wanted it, and if someone argued, they were wrong. Not him.

She'd been wrong often. But she hadn't told him how she'd felt.

She slid behind the wheel, then left the farm. Dust swirled in her wake. Gravel crunched under her tires. A sense of freedom washed over her. She was her own woman. No Tom or Reuben to stand in her way.

A single lady. And it was time she found her own happy.

Not at a bar, but that was a job. She drove across Eerie, passing the woods, the lake with light sparkling on the water and so peaceful. She'd never been much of a nature lover, but she appreciated the solitude and ability to get lost in the woods to center herself.

She continued to the east end of town. Most residents hated the east end because of the rough crowd that tended to frequent the area. The bars and dance halls were there. So was the bail bondsman's office.

She parked in the lot behind the bar in the staff area. The hotel stood behind the bar and seemed to groan in the late afternoon sun. She didn't know many of the vehicles, but she hadn't worked there yet. She hadn't met the gang. Being hired the day before made knowing people difficult. She left her car and locked it, then ventured into the building.

"Hi." A blond man with a dirty T-shirt stood by the kitchen sink. "First day?"

"It is." She recognized the man. The satyr. She thought his name was Stav. Or something like that. "You're here today?" She'd been warned against him.

"Always." He grinned and dried his hands. "My brother owns the bar. I'm sure Lance hired you."

"He did." The easy conversation reassured her. "He mentioned his baby brother."

"Good or bad?" A wicked glimmer filled his eyes.

"A little bit of both." She pocketed her keys and clutched her purse. "Told me to stay away from you."

"He would." The satyr shook his head, then held out a pruney hand. "I'm Preston."

"Lulu." She shook hands with him, and a sizzle

of recognition washed through her. Touching him jolted her attention. She let go and righted herself. The sizzle had to be a figment of her imagination.

"It's nice to meet you." Preston nodded. "I'll be at the door tonight."

"Like that?" She gestured to the filthy shirt.

"After a shower." He winked. "Although maybe it'll make me look tougher."

"It might." She wanted to touch him again. "I should get moving."

"If you need assistance, find me." He nodded once. "It's my job to keep everyone safe."

"I bet." She hadn't been told that, but his job wasn't an issue. She liked that someone was trying to protect the workers.

"I'll see you." He stepped around her and walked away.

An odd feeling sailed through her. Like a connection to him. She wasn't sure why. It wasn't like she knew him. She'd just met him. Oh, well. She wasn't looking for a connection. She just wanted to love and be loved. It was time to find her happy and find herself. The only way she'd do that was at home in Eerie, giving herself time.

Good thing she had plenty of time.

* * *

Preston raked his fingers through his hair. *Damn.* Lulu was one in a million. She'd managed, in one handshake, to make him forget his curse. He was just a real man, not a satyr for a while. Heady stuff.

He hustled over to the hotel behind the bar. The place was really a motel and a dump at that, but it was his home. He hated living there, but he had no roots so he didn't need anywhere exciting. The motel was like him, bland and beaten.

He was the son of Hermes and should be enjoying his life -- not condemned to living in a rathole and working at a bar. So what if his brother owned the bar? His brother wasn't cursed. Lance got all the breaks. Tall, dark, and handsome, never drunk, could chat easily with anyone, had women fall for him left and right. He never had to worry about being alone. People came just to see Lance. They were all pals.

Preston unlocked his door, then ventured into his room. He kept his place clean, but nothing could hide the ravages of age in the furnishings. The hotel was at least fifty years old with no renovations over those years. The place was basic.

He sat on the bed and didn't want to go back to the bar. He'd rather fish or take a drive. Maybe just listen to the birds and exist.

Preston.

He winced. *Father.* His father rarely directly showed up. That would be too easy. He instead visited Preston in his mind. *Yes?*

You have a job to do.

I know. Seduce the women at the bar. It wasn't a fun job, if he were to be honest. He hated it. Why? Because most of the women at the bar weren't interested in being with a satyr. They considered him gross. A freak. Unkempt. He tried to get his hair to cooperate, but it never worked.

As for his appearance, he'd lose the curse if he found the right girl. Like she really existed. He doubted she did.

There will be plenty of women there tonight. Lovely ones, ones to entice with wine and song, his father said. *You know what to do.*

He did and he'd long tired of the game. *I do.*

Then do it. You keep wasting time. You forgot the

bargain, didn't you?

No, he remembered it just fine. Find a woman who could love him, that they would fall for each other, without having to risk losing her to his father -- if all that happened, then he'd break the curse.

Maybe he'd find a girl who liked hooves. Or Hades would visit tonight and take him to the Underworld. That might be easier.

I'll do it. Like Preston said he would every night.

Very good. I need more playmates. Just as quickly as he'd arrived, Hermes severed the communication.

He groaned. It must be nice to have such power.

Time to ignore his father's demands again. He didn't need power, not when he simply wanted love. There wasn't a chance in Hades he'd be freed from the curse, so why even try?

He undressed and turned on the water in the shower. He couldn't remember the last time he'd been accepted for himself. He stepped under the spray. His body ached. Not just his muscles, but his soul. His core. He washed his hair, then scrubbed the rest of him before rinsing.

He hated being a satyr. Who wanted a man with horns? Hell, not only that, but who wanted to be with a man with goat's legs? It wasn't sexy. He'd been called a goat-fucker. He'd never fucked a damn goat. He was a damn freak. He didn't bother to look in the mirror any longer. There wasn't much to see.

He rinsed again, then turned the shower off. If he remembered right, he had to be back to the bar by seven. As with every night, he was expected to eye the door. He wasn't a bouncer, although he had the strength for it. He was just another observer.

Find pretty women and entice them with his jokes, sing a few songs along with the karaoke and be jovial. If she showed interest, then keep things going. It was the worst kind of life. Be a flirt. Pass the women off to his father. Nothing serious.

He dried off, then dressed before brushing his hair. It was no use. The curls went asunder as it dried. No gel could tame it. Then again, the unruliness kept his horns hidden. He wore boots to hide his hooves. If no one could see his imperfections, then they might overlook them.

He checked his look in the mirror without looking at his face. White shirt, blue vest, chains from his belt loop to his wallet, jeans, thick bracelets on his wrists and a necklace around his neck. His tattoo was barely visible under the sleeve of the shirt. His brother said the vest looked silly. He believed it gave him power and made him look tough. Who cared if it did or didn't?

He spritzed on cologne before tucking his wallet and phone into his pockets. He clipped his keys onto the same chain connected to his wallet, then locked the room before leaving. Time to go to the grind.

He hustled across the parking lot to the bar. Music already blared out to the patio area. The house band had already taken the stage. They'd ask him to sing with them a bit and he'd do it. It was his nature to sing and entertain. Wine, women and song. He might even play the guitar.

He headed into the kitchen. The scent of fried food hung thick in the air. He crinkled his nose. He hated fried anything. The faster he left the kitchen, the better. He hurried out to the bar. Patrons filled the establishment. The place was loud and full of dancers, too.

"You're here," Lance said. "Thought you'd begged off."

"No." He faced his brother. Lance had their father's good looks and his charm, too. Women loved Lance. The guy knew how to talk to women and besides, he didn't have goat legs. Preston didn't know how to charm anyone. He relied on his singing voice.

"You okay?" Lance dried a tallboy glass. "You seem tired."

"Dad contacted me." He slid his hands into his pockets. "Same story, different day."

"I know." Lance frowned. "You do seem different, though. Sad almost."

"I'm here to snag Dad a bride. What's there to hate?"

"It's not right."

"It's my fault." He'd fallen for the wrong woman and thought his father would understand. Nope. Father took Denice and cursed him. Never argue with Father.

Denice was supposed to have been worth it, but she'd ended up falling for Hermes and the allure of being with a God. Of course, she did. Why have a freak when you can have the best?

He spied Lulu. Her sweetness would be the death of him. She seemed so out of place at the bar. A bright spot in the darkness.

"Hands off Lu." Lance elbowed him. "I'm asking her out tonight."

"Can't she have a choice?" Lance got all the girls and she might not want him. Might not want Preston, either.

"Why? I'm the best here." Lance grinned. "Try for Suzie or Carla."

No, thanks. "I'll be at the door."

"I told her about your job -- you working for Hermes in procurement. Warned her, really. Keep that in mind." Lance resumed washing glasses.

"I will." Their father could be a dick. So full of himself and determined to have any woman he chose. Everyone should do what he wanted, too. Most did. But his brother could be an equally big dick, too.

He brushed past Lulu on his way to the door. "Sorry."

"Don't be." She winked. "I'm glad you're back."

"Me, too." He gasped at the electricity in her touch. His skin tingled.

"See you?" she asked.

"You will." He forced himself the rest of the way to the door. Holy Hades. He'd never felt like this before. He was drawn to her and desired Lulu. He had to forget her. He took his post with Daniel. "Hi."

"Hi. I see you noticed the new girl," Daniel said. "She's cute."

"She is." He wanted to kiss her.

"Lance has his sights set on her."

"He does."

"She's not his type."

"Nope." She was too nice.

"Might be yours," Daniel said. "She really grinned at you."

"Nah." Did she? He'd missed it.

"Keep an eye on her. She's special." Daniel marked the wrists of the women entering the bar with a stamp.

Preston nodded. He didn't get any odd vibe from the women. A few men arrived as well. His senses tingled. Something about the men felt off. He had a good sixth sense when it came to troublemakers and these guys set it off. All three were handsome and self-centered, but that struck him as odd because while they acted cocky, they were too overt about it. Like they should have anyone there.

He'd have to keep an eye on them. He didn't want trouble or for someone to treat the other patrons like shit. Eerie and the bar might be places for paras to disappear, but that didn't mean someone should disappear for good. He stepped into the bar and watched the men. He might not be able to snag women for his father tonight, but if he could stop trouble before it started, then he'd have done his job.

Chapter Two

Lulu cleared the table and placed the glasses in the bus tub. Her feet ached and she hadn't known this level of exhaustion in so long. At least she had plenty of tip money for her efforts.

"Hey, baby." A male strode up to her and his eyes sparkled. "What's a pretty girl like you doing here?"

She crooked her brow. What a terrible pick-up line. "Working."

"If you were my girl, you wouldn't be working," he said. "You'd be a queen."

"There's already a queen." She wiped the table. "I'm not her."

"You should be."

He'd smeared it on a bit thick. "Uh-huh."

He leaned in close enough for his breath to tickle her ear. "I could make you queen."

"No, thanks." She picked up the tub. "I'm needed in the kitchen."

He stepped into her path. "Fine."

"Fine, what? I need to go." She held up the tub. "To take these to the dishwasher."

The sparkle in his eye changed. "I know what you are."

"Oh?" She wasn't even sure, so she'd love to hear this. "Do tell."

"You're a rare magical being. The powers of a witch and an elf." He leered at her. "Dangerous."

Considering she had no powers… he was way off. She laughed and shook her head. "You're serious?"

"I am."

She rolled her eyes. "Stop."

He grabbed her wrist. "You need to stop

blocking me."

Huh?

He yanked her wrist, causing her to lose control of the tub.

"Stop!" The contents spilled onto the floor and glass shattered everywhere. Great. Now she'd have to pick this all up. The fool.

"Now." He pinched her wrist, leaving a mark.

"Hi." Preston stepped between her and the man. "I need a drink. Do you have a drink?" He wobbled, pushing into the man and allowing her freedom.

Lulu abandoned the tub and ducked around Preston to the safety of the kitchen. Once the man was gone, she'd clean up the mess. Her heart hammered. What in the hell had just happened?

Preston joined her a few moments later at the dishwasher. "Are you okay?"

"Yeah." She loaded the soap into the machine. "Thanks. I thought I had that, but he gained strength as he grabbed me." She hadn't even looked at her wrist. It ached and she feared what she'd find when she looked at it.

"He did."

She shook her head. "I can handle myself."

"I know you can, but he's a sorcerer."

She hadn't run into many of those. "What?"

"He was trying to infiltrate your mind."

"Why?" She closed the lid on the machine and hit the button to start it. "He wanted to get some?"

"Of your energy."

She frowned. "Please."

"I'm serious."

"Why would he want that?"

"Because you have the power of the witches in you and the determination of the elves, but you don't look like either. Most children of the elves, no matter what the other parent is, look like elves. You look like everyone else."

"So I'm a freak?" She wasn't shocked. She'd heard it a thousand times.

"You're more powerful."

"Than a freak?"

"Than you think."

"Come on."

"He targeted you for a reason. He wants to consume your power."

"That's nuts." But not completely shocking, either.

"It's what they do. He looks young, but it's a false front. He's an old sorcerer looking for younger power to keep him alive."

She stared at Preston. He was either smarter than he looked or one hell of a manipulator.

"It's true. Ask Lance."

He wouldn't reference his brother without reason. "Why should I trust you?"

"I have nothing to lose other than my teeth." He shrugged. "I want to help you."

She hesitated again. "I appreciate it." She could use all the help she could get. "What should I do? I have to clean up the mess."

"Delilah got it. Used her magic." He shrugged. "She's a full witch and they don't want her magic."

"Lovely." She rested her hands on her hips. She'd have to thank Delilah later. "Then what do I do?"

"Get a partner. Now."

"You? The satyr working for Hermes wants me to find a partner? That's rich." She laughed, amused with him but knowing he wasn't right.

"Ask Lance. Pair up with Lance, I don't care. Just be careful." Preston walked away, leaving her at the washing station.

Blunt. He hadn't pushed her, either. Well, shit. She drummed her fingers on the machine. He had a point. She might not know her full capabilities, but until she did, she needed help.

Lance strolled into the kitchen. "You're in here."

"I am." She regained her composure. "I got hit on and needed a second."

"Play up to it. Jesus. Get better tips from them and make them drink more," Lance said. "We're here to make money."

"We are." Jerk. He didn't give a shit about her safety. Good thing she wasn't attracted to him. He'd make a terrible partner. But she needed someone to help her.

"Are you in there?" Lance asked. "I hired a waitress, not a statue."

"Sorry." She snapped to attention and rushed out of the kitchen to the main bar. She had to work, or she'd never get her rent paid. The tips were good, but she had to keep going.

"There you are." The sorcerer stepped into her path. "You will come home with me."

"I --" How did he have a hold on her mind already? She hadn't opened to him.

Preston rushed up to her. "Babe."

She flicked her attention to Preston. "Yes?"

"I have your wallet." Preston touched her elbow. "You left it at home."

"Thank you for bringing it up, my love." She kissed him. Her lips tingled. It was too easy to call him her love. Felt right, too.

Preston grinned. "You know I expect more

payment."

He was good at this. "You'll get it." She winked. "Always do."

"I know it." Preston frowned "Am I interrupting something?"

"No." The sorcerer turned on his heel and left.

She sighed. "Thanks. You saved my ass."

"Not yet. He's still around." Preston steered her to the kitchen. "I'll do this for you but be careful. He got into your mind, didn't he?"

"He did." She lowered her voice. "How do I combat him? With you?"

"If that's what you want, we'll do it. I won't force you, but you need to prove to him we're together."

"Then we will." No question.

"Lulu."

She wasn't convincing enough? Fine. "I kissed you. I didn't do that out of compassion. I did it because I wanted to." How could she make him understand?

"You did?"

"So that doesn't mean anything? I'm attracted to you."

"You do realize who I am, right? The man you mentioned earlier? I'm supposed to get women for my father, Hermes. Most people don't want to hook up with a guy who might toss them over to dear old Dad."

"You might, but I doubt it. If you were going to do that, you've have been more covert about it than you are."

"True. I could be king."

"You could've told me crap to get me into Daddy's arms. You didn't. You saved my butt."

He groaned. "You don't understand."

"No, I don't." She needed to hide from Lance and the sorcerer. "Tell me."

"Women don't fall for me -- even if it's fake."

"Because you're a satyr?"

"Among other things."

He annoyed her. "You don't trust people."

"Would you?"

"No."

"Well, then."

"Pres, stop. I want to be with you. Not because of my predicament or because I think you'll turn me over to Hermes. I'm drawn to you. You fascinate me." It was the total truth. It was happening rather fast, but she wasn't in a position to argue.

"I do?"

"You do." She grasped his hand. Tingles shot through her like electricity. She couldn't breathe for a second. She'd never felt this way before.

"You need to be sure this is what you want," he said. "I'm serious."

"I do."

He groaned again. "Lulu, you'll be forced to decide if you want to be with me or him."

"Who him?"

"Hermes."

She snorted. "Why? I don't even have a spark with him. So what if he's your Dad? He's not my type." She hadn't met him and doubted he would be.

"Lu."

"I don't want a sorcerer or a god. I want to try my luck with you." If he could protect her, then she'd go with him just about anywhere. "Truly."

"You'll regret it."

"I really doubt it." For once, she knew better. She'd chosen the right path, and now it was just a matter of figuring out where it'd go.

* * *

Preston hid his discomfort. He'd broken the rule his brother had set, and he'd grabbed the attention away from his father by being with her. Lulu was adorable and hard to forget. She'd be the perfect fodder for Hermes.

What was worse? Preston liked her.

And she'd kissed him.

She hadn't pushed. He hadn't pushed.

Well, not really.

He managed to get through the rest of the night but kept a close eye on Lulu. He'd incur the wrath of his brother, but part of him didn't care. He'd piss off his father, too. That didn't matter. Right now, she did.

At the end of the night, long after the sorcerers finally left, he stopped Lulu. "Hey."

"Hi." She counted up her tips. "I had a good night."

"Good." He crossed his ankles and leaned on the bar. "Made a lot?"

"I did." She grinned. "How about you?"

"It's been good." He didn't know what to do. He didn't want to push her, but she'd need his help sooner than later.

"You look odd." She tucked the money into her apron. "We should talk."

"Nah. I'll escort you to your car, though." He slipped his hands into his pockets and moved away from the bar.

"I can manage this myself." She trailed after him. "Pres. We need to talk."

"Lu, we don't. I know you've got reservations and it's fine." He'd be okay.

"What?" She touched his arm. "Pres. Wait."

He slowed his steps as he entered the kitchen. "Yeah?"

"I'm not having second thoughts, if that's what you think."

He had to be dreaming. Women didn't want him. "Because of the magic. I get it."

"I don't think you do." She turned him around. "Truly."

"Lu."

"Come to the apartment tonight. I get my keys tonight and I've got to get used to being there, but I don't want to go alone." She grasped his hand. "I'm not interested in being alone tonight. We should talk. Please?"

He wanted to turn her down. Wanted to walk away from her because he feared she'd reject him.

"You need to protect me, and we should play up the story, right?"

Ah, that. "Yeah." This was just protection. He could handle that.

"We've never been alone together, and we need a plan." She squeezed his fingers. "Besides, you're my friend. I'd like to thank you for helping me. You didn't have to jump in the way you did."

"I'm a good guy."

"You are." Her grin intensified. "But you're also a guy with a big heart. Most guys would be rushing to my place right now and you're not. That shows you're honorable and also that you're the kind of guy I want to know."

Every cell in his body screamed for her. His magic called to her. He should just go. No thinking, just go.

"Please?" She held on tighter. "I've got a whopper of a story for you, and you need to know."

He nodded. "Okay." He'd have to protect his heart, but he could do it. She deserved the best, which wasn't him.

"Shit." She winced. "The magic is here."

"What?" He hadn't felt a different charge.

"The magic. The mood is different." She shivered. "I can't tell what it is."

"Stay here." He peeked out into the dining room. The place was dark and deserted. When he returned to the kitchen, Lance stood by the door.

"Damn sorcerers." Lance pounded his fist on the doorframe. "What in the hell?"

Preston stepped between Lulu and the door. He spotted the sorcerers from earlier in the evening. "Damn it."

"You know them?" Lance asked.

"I served them," Lulu said.

"And I tried to trail them," Preston said. He'd messed up when he let them leave.

"They're back." Lance kept his back to Preston. "Must be some very special magic here. Something pure."

"Not me." Lulu grasped Preston's hand again. "Why are they doing this?"

"Sorcerers love trouble." Lance sighed. "Damn fools."

He hadn't expected such a deep thought from his brother. Lance actually sounded concerned for a change. "I know what it is," Preston said. "I know what they want."

Lance finally turned around. "What?"

"Her." Preston glanced at Lulu. "Her magic drew them."

"I'm not special," she whispered.

"Are to them," Lance said.

"I partnered with Preston. That saves me, right?" She tucked into Preston. "We're doing something."

"You and my brother?" Lance's brows rose. "Pres?"

"Yes." He wanted to groan. Jesus H. Christ on a cracker. "It's very new."

"So?" Lulu clutched his arm.

"Not what I expected you to say or what I expected to hear." Lance frowned. "Could've picked me."

"I could have." She kept a hold on Preston. "What do we do?"

Like he knew? He needed to think.

"You can't take her to that ratbag motel you live in," Lance said. "It's a dump."

"Thank you." How irritating. "We need to go anywhere but here."

"My place." She grabbed his hand. "If they want my magic, then they'll have to find me."

"They will," Lance said. "Go, and I'll cover for you."

Preston hated that this was happening, but he needed to keep her safe. "Let's go."

She hurried with him to the parking lot to her car.

"Where…" No, he'd ask later. He grabbed her keys from her hand and unlocked the vehicle before jumping behind the wheel.

She joined him in the car. "I can drive."

"I know you can, but they're looking for my weakness. If I'm not being an alpha, they'll doubt me and attack you." They'd attack regardless, but this bought him some time. The car sped out of the lot, slinging gravel. "Sorry."

"I need new tires anyway." She held tight to her purse and apron. "To the bakery. I live above *Whipped Up*."

"Nice." He hurried through town to her building. He liked the place, but he'd never be welcomed there. Not without her beside him. Most people didn't want a satyr in their presence.

"Go into the parking garage behind the building. Second floor." She pointed to the entrance. "No one will know, but that's where my spot's supposed to be."

"Supposed to?" He drove through the structure to the second level. "There's only four spots."

"I'm the middle one. Everyone else in the building is up on the third floor -- more room."

He parked and switched off the engine. "I'm sorry."

"You're sorry? It's two in the morning and I still need to get the keys. They weren't ready at three when I was here last. We need to hit the office first." She tucked her purse and apron under her arm. "Let's go."

He trailed her into the building to the desk. He'd only been to the bakery once and never upstairs. The Old World atmosphere and antique quality of the space charmed him. The place oozed class. Carved wood, textured wallpaper, thick carpeting and not a speck of dust. "Wow."

"I know. It's pretty great." She rushed up to the desk. "Hey, Gladys. How's things?"

"Good." Gladys left her seat and pushed a key across the counter. "Sorry. We were getting it cleaned for you."

"Not a problem." She signed the paperwork, then accepted the key.

"Filled the fridge and cupboards, too. Figured you'd need it." Gladys grinned, then her smile fell. "Oh, you."

"Hi, Gladys." He'd met her a couple times and she hadn't liked him much. He'd also been pretending to be drunk so he could be the center of the party. "How are you?"

"Are you staying with her?" Gladys eyeballed him. The color of her hair changed from purple to fiery red. "Is this someone special?"

Lulu sighed and shook her head. "I hope it won't be a problem. He's my special friend."

"I see." Gladys dipped her head. "Just don't bring others of your kind here. We keep the place classy."

His kind. Fucking balls.

"Gladys." Lulu shook her head. "Come on. He's a good guy. I wouldn't bring anyone here who's not."

"Just know they aren't the best kind of friend." Gladys clicked her tongue. "Be on your guard."

"I will." She grasped Preston's hand. "Thank you."

Preston wanted to melt into the floor. Normally, he'd act ballsy and ignore the comments, but he liked Lulu and didn't like the impression Gladys gave. Sure, some of the satyrs could be dickheads. Some of the centaurs could, the vampires were worse, and the shifters were the most dangerous. So what?

He followed along with her to the apartment door. "This is yours?"

"Guess so." She shrugged and let go. "I've never been here before. Just saw photos online." She unlocked the door and stepped back, giving him first view.

"In case there's something bad here?" He ventured in first. He didn't spot anything bad, but he wasn't sure what might be out of order. He'd never been there, either. As he walked from room to room, he checked the magic and nodded. Nothing terrible. "It's clear."

"Good." She darted in and locked the door. "Fuck."

"Dirty mouth." He hadn't expected her to swear.

"I do it when I'm stressed." She sighed. "It's not a good habit."

"Doesn't matter." He debated kicking out of his boots, then declined. She didn't need to see his hooves. "Holy shit."

"You've said it." She tossed her apron on the counter. "We need to sort us out."

No kidding. "Look, we don't have to really be together. We just need to sell the lie."

"Hold up." She held her hands out. "I mean, we need to decide what to do next."

"Yeah." He couldn't think straight. He wanted to be with someone who cared about him, but didn't want to hide, either.

"Okay." She crossed the minuscule kitchen to the fridge and opened the door. She withdrew two bottles of beer. "She said she'd stocked it. I'm impressed."

He leaned on the door frame. "She's true to her word."

"She is. I picked this apartment because it's furnished. Gladys wasn't going to rent it, but when I said I had nothing, she was a little more agreeable. She knew my mother." She popped the tops on the bottles. "Have one."

"Nice." He'd never heard of anyone renting a furnished apartment outside of the motel.

"Sit. We should talk and strategize."

"We should." He wandered over to the couch. "Thanks."

She sat on the other end of the sofa. "Have a seat and kick off your boots."

"I shouldn't." He hated the look of his hooves.

"Afraid your feet are stinky? I don't care." She shrugged. "I might be able to create a spell to get rid of the stench."

"No." He didn't want to look at his malady. "I have hooves, remember?" Jesus Christ. He hoped that hadn't made her change her mind. His heart wouldn't survive. He already liked her.

Chapter Three

She stared at him. He was a satyr. Of course, he'd have hooves. She knew that. "Okay?"

"You're not upset?"

"No. Why should I be? I'm a freak. I refuse to insult someone else." She took a drag from the bottle of beer. The tart brew burned the back of her throat and chilled her to her soul. Yes, she needed a clear head to deal with the situation, but she needed to relax, too.

"You're not a freak." He downed a large draw from his bottle. "I am."

"Then we both are." No point in arguing. "So?"

"I keep hoping you'll come to your senses. I'm a satyr. I'm bad for you, even if I did volunteer to help you. I said I would and I will."

"You're really messed up by that -- being a satyr." She peeled at the label. "You shouldn't see it as a liability. It's an asset."

His eyes widened.

"I'll bet you've never heard that before, have you?" She peeled the paper from the bottle. "I know freaks. Trust me. You're not one."

"What do you know?" He snorted. "You've probably had life go your way."

"No." She held up her hand. God, she hated her life, but she didn't want the burden alone. "I didn't live a charmed life. I had to work for what I got. My mother, as you know, is a witch and my father is an elf. I look like neither of them. I got teased because I didn't have magic, not much."

He didn't argue, as she'd expected. Instead, he listened. "Sorry."

"See? Just because you think something about someone doesn't make it true."

"No."

"You're a good guy. You're original, and that's pretty sweet. I like original."

He grinned. "Then it's a good thing I am."

"You are," she said. "I have to confess, tonight wasn't my first encounter with sorcerers. I dated one for a while. Not one of those guys. His name was Reuben. I didn't know why I was so attracted to him so fast or why I needed him that much. By the time I realized what he'd done, it was too late. He'd begun to use me. He had me completely convinced he was the only man I ever needed. Everything I did was wrong and I needed to change myself."

"Christ." His eyes widened again. "He knew you had magic you hadn't tapped."

"He did, but I had no idea. I'm still not sure what to think, but I know he used me. He had me so messed up."

"What made you leave? You got away."

She nodded. "I decided I couldn't be wrong all the time." A chuckle bubbled in her throat. "If there was a problem, he claimed I caused it. He was automatically right, and me? I was wrong. I used the desire to finally have the truth to break free. I picked up my stuff -- whatever I could carry -- and left. Just walked out."

"Did he follow?" He sat on the edge of the cushion. He hadn't touched the beer since the first swig.

"I'm sure he's still looking for me." She tried to shrug to hide her fear. "I worry he'll find me, but I never said I lived here. I said I came from New York." She hated lying to anyone, but Reuben had deserved it. Besides, the lie bought her time.

"He'll find you."

"He will." She shrugged again to hide her concern. "He found another woman, but she proved to be less than he expected. He thought she'd be the love of his life. Had plenty of magic, could charm him and treated him well, but she turned out to be a liar, a cheater -- imagine that -- and had stronger magic than him. She nearly destroyed him. I wish she had." Would've kept him from trying to find her.

He frowned. "That explains why he wouldn't stay with her."

"It does. He swore he'd get me back to make me see it was a mistake. I didn't want him, but that never stopped him before." She hated to admit that. The less she remembered, the better. "Think he might have sent them?"

"Could've." Preston sighed and fiddled with the bottle. "Look, I don't know how to help you. Not really. I deal with drunks, magic that's not nearly as strong, and annoyances at the bar. People who want to cause trouble."

"You can help me, though?" Shit. She hadn't considered he might change his mind once he got her alone.

"I can, but only if we're truly supposed to be together. Your magic is mine and mine is yours." He shook his head. "I can't expect that from you."

"You can." How could she get him to make sense of this? She moved over to him, brushing her knee against his. "I want to explore this."

"Us?"

"Yes." She put the bottle down. "If we have to be a couple to put them off, then we will."

"Even if you don't like me?"

"Who said I don't like you?" She slipped her hand into his. "You know a lot of my story and didn't back away. That's huge." She hadn't told him everything, but still.

"It'd be a joke."

She groaned. "So what? Even a joke could become real. You never know. What if I want the chance to explore this?" To explore *him;* not that she could say that now.

"Are you sure?"

"Very." She crawled onto his lap and threaded her arms around his neck. She straddled him. Heat overwhelmed her and she could barely breathe. He smelled good. Something within her vibrated. She wasn't sure what the hell was doing it or why. She'd never felt this way before.

She met his gaze. The liquid blue of his irises mesmerized her. She sucked in a ragged breath.

"Hi." He smoothed his palms over her thighs. "Uh… damn."

"Don't like what you see?" She toyed with the curls at the base of his skull. He had the softest hair.

"I do," he said, his voice husky.

"Then take it. I'm ready." More than ready. She'd never been this needy before. Her nipples beaded and liquid lust pooled low in her belly. She needed to be touched. She craved him and the desire overwhelmed her.

He cleared his throat. "Jesus."

"Not interested?" She swore her skin would burn off. "Pres?"

"Are you sure you aren't part shifter?" he asked and cocked his head.

"No, why?" Why would he ask that?

"You're giving off serious pheromones." He groaned. "Holy fuck."

"You don't want me." Why didn't he? He should

be carrying her to the bedroom, yet he wasn't.

"Your eyes are glowing." He slid his hands along her ribs. "Like a shifter."

That gave her pause. "What?" She'd never been told her eyes glowed. It didn't feel like they were.

"They're deep green. A moment ago, they were blue." He tipped his head. "It's beautiful."

"Thanks?" She shrank back from him. "You don't want me." She knew rejection when she saw it.

"It's not that." He caressed her ribs with his thumbs. "I do."

"Then take me."

"Not like this."

She didn't understand. The connection and desire seemed to be there.

"You're displaying mating heat."

She stared at him, confused. "Mating heat?" She wasn't a shifter.

"It happens when paranormals are with someone special." He tensed. "I don't know. I'm not special."

"Neither am I."

"Which is why I'm concerned it's wonky. It's misfiring because of that sorcerer's draining, maybe? The sorcerers messed with your magic, too, so that could be part of it. You're messed up."

She didn't like the sound of that. She'd been told she was messed up and broken before. He had no idea. "I'm sorry?"

"Honey, you don't even know your magic, do you?" he asked. "I'd like for you to get ahold of it before we do the deed -- if we do. You'll change your mind."

"If?" She'd change her mind? What balls!

"Yeah." He shrugged. "It'll probably happen."

"So that's it? You're unreal. I kissed you. I'm

attracted to you." Why didn't he get it? Why didn't she want to push him fully away? "I want you. More than I could ever believe." Christ, more than her next breath.

He closed his eyes. "I was wrong. It's not mating heat. My father must've infiltrated your mind. That bastard must've figured out you're here, and he wants in on your magic. I knew he'd do it. That's why the sorcerers showed up. They were sent to mess you up so he can swoop in."

She didn't like the sound of any of that. This wasn't of her will? Jesus. "I'm sorry?" She wasn't sure what else to say.

"Honey, you need to get ahold of your magic -- and the Hades away from my father's influence -- so you can."

She left his lap. "I don't want anyone else, just you. Come with me." She grasped his hands and hauled him to his feet. He allowed her to tug him to the bedroom. She needed to be with him too much. No, she wanted to be naked with him and rubbing all over his body. If she wasn't careful, she'd claw her clothes right off.

He gathered her in his arms but didn't kiss her. He didn't push, either. He simply held her and petted her hair.

Tears sprang in her eyes. What was happening? She wished she could make sense of it all. He should be fucking her.

Using her.

Taking what he wanted.

Controlling.

He wasn't.

He held her to his chest and sat on the bed. "It'll be okay. I'm here and the magic he's using will pass." He kept petting her hair. "It'll be okay. The magic is directing you, not you."

What? Magic directing her... again. She didn't fight him, but damn. This wasn't of her own will. How fucked up.

"I've got you, honey. I promise I won't let you go." He kissed the top of her head.

She believed him. Despite the overwhelming desire to be with him, she trusted that he'd told her the truth. He'd been a gentleman. For a satyr, that was supposed to be huge.

She needed to be with him, though, with or without the magic. He was the one. Her one.

* * *

Preston stretched out on the bed and held her. Damn his father's magic. Preston wanted her to love him, not fear him or go stark raving because of the magic and his father's pushing. She had to love him for him. Not because of mating pheromones.

She curled up against him and slept. He knew the moment she gave in to slumber because she grew heavy against his chest. She curled her hand on his belly.

He should let go of her and take her shoes off. Should leave her alone, too. Should get the hell out of her bedroom. Except he'd promised he'd keep her safe. Promised he'd be with her. Not that being with her was a hardship. Hell, she'd marked him with her scent. He wore it proudly. She had his on her, too. Marked his heart as well, but he couldn't tell her that.

You've picked out a good one, Hermes said, infiltrating Preston's mind. *She's pretty, but sweet, too.*

He gritted his teeth. She wasn't there for his father's taking. *No.* At least he could respond through his mind. *She's not available.*

Seems like she is.

Sorry. He didn't tend to defy his father often, but he needed to be with her tonight.

Sorry? You'd disobey me?

He snorted. It was time he did. She deserved no less. *Yes.*

You will deliver her to me tonight. I will have her. That magic is strong and pure. It's pristine. Hermes laughed. *She will fit in my collection well.*

Pristine magic? She thought she'd been damaged. He shook his head.

With the magic of the elves and that of the witch, she's very powerful. Can't you see that? Hermes growled. *Silly satyr. You'll never learn.*

He could see a lot more than he let on, but he wanted his father to leave her and her magic alone. She did have something powerful within her, but no idea how to use it. The sorcerers wanted her magic and he now understood why. She had power and didn't look like either of her parents, which meant she had more magic than some minor gods. She was the perfect mix. A rare jewel.

You will deliver her tonight to me. The mating magic is within her and she's ripe, Hermes said. *She wants to be the mistress of the god.*

Uh-huh. Like Hades he'd allow that to happen. But he appreciated knowing it was mating magic, the strongest magic.

She will be mine.

Good luck with that. He refused to let his father win. If she wanted Hermes, he'd back down, but only if she made the choice. He closed his mind to his father, something he rarely did. He squeezed his eyes shut and held her tight. He'd never wanted something more than Lulu.

One day she might actually like him, too. Not

with mating magic, but a real connection. He closed his eyes and relaxed. She'd imprinted him with her scent. She might not know it yet, but she'd chosen him. Fuck. He'd never be the same. She could be the one. Fuckety fuck. He shouldn't be allowing himself to get too close to her, but it'd happened. He'd have to play the part.

He slipped off to sleep, despite his need to stay awake. He needed to be vigilant, but rest called him.

She curled tighter into him. "No."

He woke immediately. Sunlight filled the room and he blinked. What the fuck?

A figure stood in the room, their face blocked by the sunlight behind them.

Lulu trembled. "Who are you? Why are you in my home?"

He sat up, putting himself between her and the figure. "Are you going to play games?"

The figure disappeared, leaving no trace of their existence.

She shook harder. "What just happened?"

He pinched the bridge of his nose. He knew what he'd seen and cursed himself for not noticing faster. "A guard from my father's realm, that's who showed up." He hadn't been visited by the Guardians in so long. Having one of them show up wasn't good. "They're sizing you up."

"Who?" She scurried off the bed. "I'm still dressed."

"You are." He flattened his boots on the floor. "My father noticed you."

"Good for him." She wrapped her arms around her body. "Not interested."

"I told him that." He reached for her. "Come here."

She crept up to him. "What's going on?"

"You and I have formed a bond."

"We did."

It wasn't a question. He sighed. "Just..." He shook his head. He'd jacked this up so much and she deserved better. "I will protect you with my life."

Her eyes widened. "Pres? You've changed your mind?"

"I did." He couldn't let her down. Not any longer. "You should have a better man than me. One who's not cursed. But the magic chose us for each other. The magic knows and I won't question that."

"So what do we do?"

She seemed so unbothered by the whole situation. Her coolness would kill him. "You're not upset?"

"Not by you. The jerk infiltrating my room freaks me out, but I trusted you had this in hand." She threaded her arms around his waist. "I don't know anything about curses, but I know I'm drawn to you."

"We need time."

"We do." She rested her head on his shoulder and caressed his ribs. "I never said I'm in love with you or that I want to seal the pairing. I'm drawn."

"You did say that." He rubbed his cheek on her hair.

"I want the chance to see where this goes. Yes, we need to sell to the sorcerers and the rest of the world that we're fine and should be left alone, but that doesn't mean we can't enjoy our time together. We can." She tensed in his arms. "Right?"

"Right." He'd jumped right into the line of losing his heart to her, but whatever. Losing his heart wasn't all that bad.

"Right?" She grinned. "I'm scared as shit. Don't tease me."

"No teasing." He kissed her temple and his lips tingled. He should've given in to her right away. He liked her too much and holding her pleased him. She brought out his desire to protect her and be more than a naughty satyr.

"Thank you." She relaxed a bit. "I never thought my life would get this far out of control. Not again."

"It'll be okay." He'd protect her -- from the sorcerers, her past, his father... everything -- even if it killed him. He'd figure something out to make this work. He had to. Her life depended on it.

Chapter Four

Lulu cleared the table and tucked the money into her apron pocket. Preston had moved in with her the previous week and she'd spent so much time with him. The best time, but instead of sex like she'd expected, he'd made her wait. She'd never been with a man who hadn't treated her like a sex object.

To be honest, the change pleased her. It also scared her to death. Didn't he find her attractive? He seemed to, but she worried he'd want her as a fake partner and nothing more. She wanted this to be real.

She caught Preston's gaze and he winked. A rush of heat surged through her. Fire settled low in her belly. No one else made her feel this way. He'd mentioned the mating magic, which freaked her out. Maybe her attraction to him wasn't real. That scared her even more.

"Lu?" Lance nodded to her. "Can I see you in the office?"

"Sure. Let me drop this off." She carried the tray to the kitchen and left the plates at the dishwashing station. She deposited the tray in the holder, then rushed to the office. She hadn't wiped the table before she left the dining room. Damn.

"Lu." Lance sat on the edge of the desk. "You seem distracted."

"I do?" It showed that much? "I'm sorry."

"Slow down. You don't need to be sorry." He held up both hands. "I didn't mean to upset you."

"If I'm not doing my job, then please let me know." She'd jumped to a huge conclusion, but the words tumbled out.

"You're getting ahead of yourself and off topic." Lance sighed. Pain resonated in his eyes. "I don't think you're not doing your job."

"Then what?" She should stop talking. Should be out there taking care of her tables, really.

"I wanted to ask you if you're okay. You seem distracted. Is my brother bothering you?" Lance asked.

"No."

"He's being a gentleman?"

"Yes." What else would he be?

"Can we talk?" Lance asked. "Civil talk?"

"Sure." She didn't know why she couldn't sit still. "Sorry."

"You're wound up."

"I know."

"Want to tell me why?"

Her annoyance grew, but mostly with herself. She thought she excelled at hiding her emotions.

"If it's Preston, please tell me. He can be a lot." Lance cocked his head. "I can tell you honestly enjoy his company."

"I've been around him a lot beyond here at the bar and I do. I'm drawn to him, but it's tricky."

He frowned. "Tricky?"

She had to tell someone. "The first night, I wanted to lick him and crawl all over him. Like nothing held me back, I wanted it so much." She'd given away too much information, but he had to understand. Maybe he could explain it better.

"But?"

"He said it was mating magic. Have you ever heard of mating magic?"

He nodded. "That's a good thing. He needs to be accepted, so if the magic within you wants him, then that's awesome."

"No, the connection was magic. Mating magic." Why wasn't he listening?

"I want a magical connection with someone, so I'm not seeing the problem."

"The magic got a hold of me -- like with the sorcerers. It wasn't right." God. She sounded so lame. She'd been taken over again. That's what it had to be.

"Wait. I heard you, but thought you'd confused the term. Mating magic?"

"Yes." How many times did she have to say it? "Never mind. It's nothing."

"That's not nothing."

"Don't worry about it." She didn't want to discuss this any longer.

"Uh, you do need to worry." Lance rounded her, then closed the office door. "If the mating magic caught you, then the connection to Preston is real."

"That's what he said." She folded her arms. "So?" She liked the sound of the connection being real.

"I don't know the whole story with your kind of magic. Every paranormal is a little different, but I have the feeling he understands. He's smart that way." Lance hooked his fingers in his jeans pockets. "What I do know is that when the mating magic strikes, it's correct. It's true."

"Is it?" She tensed. Then why wasn't Preston trying to be with her?

"But you're scared. I can see it in your eyes." He dipped his head once. "What scares you?"

She hesitated. The magic did freak her out. "Okay, he says he'll protect me and that he's drawn to me, but he barely touches me. Like he's disgusted. Or he's afraid. Did I do something wrong?"

"No."

"Other guys have been far pushier. I've heard stories about his boldness, but I haven't seen it. He practically avoids me." She fiddled with her apron.

"What'd I do wrong?"

"You've been with the wrong guys." Lance sighed. "My brother is careful. He acts like a dick sometimes to protect himself. I give him shit because he's a satyr, but he's a stand-up guy. If he's keeping his hands to himself, then he's doing it for you. He wants you, I'm sure. Wants to make love to you right now. But he's afraid you'll change your mind."

"Why would I do that?" At least Preston had been telling her the truth. She stared at Lance. "I've never been this drawn to someone else."

"Then that's a good thing." Lance nodded. "He's had a couple other women give him the time of day, but change their mind when they learned he's a satyr. They wanted to be with our father, not him. Dad has power and Pres has hooves."

"That's fucked up." She slapped her hand over her mouth. "Sorry."

"No problem because you're right. It is," Lance said. "But it's what he deals with. He's supposed to deliver to our father whomever Dad wants for a playmate, but Preston's being used. He knows it."

"He does." Her heart broke. "How do I know it won't happen to me?"

"What do you mean?"

"How can I keep from falling for the bullshit? If there's magic involved, I'm screwed."

He shook his head. "Not really."

"Oh?" He had her interest. "I'm not good at combating magic." Lousy, really.

"Follow your heart. The magic isn't perfect, but if you really like him, keep trying." Lance crossed his ankles. "And if you need advice, find me. I want Pres to be happy. I haven't seen a spring in his step in forever. He's a changed man."

"Is he?" She liked the sound of that.

"You make him happy. Keep doing what you're doing." He winked. "And trust your gut. It's serving you well."

She nodded. "I will." She liked having an ally. She didn't feel so alone.

"Preston is a strange animal. He's so guarded. He worries he'll be used, but never that someone might be attracted to him. If you are," Lance said, "go with it."

"He's been hurt before?" The information wasn't her business, but she needed to know the truth.

"He was, a couple times. One was a lousy fit. The other had potential, but she found out she liked the attention of the Gods instead."

"Sweet gal."

"She could be. Had a thing for married men, too. If she could destroy a relationship or a person, she would do it without a second thought. Real piece of work," Lance said.

She hesitated. "Was he in love with her?" Her breath lodged in her throat. *Shit*. She hadn't meant to get so involved. She wasn't sure she wanted the answer, either.

"Not really. He thought he was, but I could see in his eyes he wasn't." Lance sighed. "That's not in his eyes right now. I see the light there."

She nodded and a smile pulled at the corners of her mouth. "I'm glad."

"You should be." He winked again. "Get back to work. Keep up what you're doing. It's good."

"Thanks." She smoothed her hands over her apron. "I will."

"Oh, one more thing. If you want to help prove your case, ask him out on a date. A real one."

She paused at the door. "What do you mean?"

"A date. Out to dance or dinner or something."

"If it's not too forward that I ask him. Some guys get strange when the woman takes charge."

"He might get touchy, but he'll be happy you asked." He grinned. "He likes forward women, especially if they're interested in him."

"I tried and he said it was just magic -- not real."

"That's his defense mechanism. He does it to keep you and everyone else at bay. Don't let him," Lance said. "The magic is true. It's a little overwhelming, so follow it, but don't give up."

She sighed again. The overwhelming thing wasn't the half of it. It made the situation so murky. But Preston deserved a chance. She liked him too much. "I will."

"The magic, even mating, isn't wrong. It knows, so let it guide you."

"To Preston?"

He nodded. "Exactly."

He had so much confidence in her. She wished she had it, too.

"Trust me. I wouldn't be this transparent with you otherwise. I know this. I do," Lance said. "I wouldn't tell you any of this if I didn't think the magic is true."

"Okay." She had to trust him. She didn't have much choice otherwise.

She left the office and headed to the main room for her tables. The table she'd left was already clean. She hadn't done it, so the other server must've done it. "Sybil?"

The faerie stopped at the table. "Yeah?"

"Thanks for cleaning this for me. I appreciate the help."

"Help? Wasn't me." Sybil shrugged. "I've been hopping since you left the floor."

"You didn't clean the table?" Then who had?

"Not me." Sybil tucked her pad into her apron. "Preston did. Must be trying to score points."

"With me?" She liked that.

"Could be. Must want to get into your panties. Or give you over to his daddy." She snorted. "Slimeball."

"What if he does want... in my panties?" She left the table to check on the others. As she finished her round, she caught Preston's gaze.

He grinned.

"Thank you." She brushed her hand across his arm. Sparks shot through her system. It didn't feel like magic -- not traditional magic. This was real and she wanted more.

"Hi, sweetheart." Preston stepped away from the door. "You look like you've seen a ghost."

"I can see them. They're real," she said and fixed her gaze on his. "I've seen them."

"So have I." His voice was low and gravelly.

Heat swirled in her belly. "Did they throw a party?"

"No." He laughed. "The ghosts didn't throw a party. What are you talking about, Lu?"

"I'm trying to make conversation." And failing. She groaned. "I hear you like to dance."

"I hate dancing." He rubbed her back. "But I like being with you."

"You do?"

"You've caught my eye."

She knew that. He wouldn't be touching her otherwise. She sucked in a ragged breath, then exhaled. "Would you like to go out somewhere with me?"

"Like where?"

"On a date. I don't know where." Her hands shook. "You and me." She'd made a mess of this.

"I live with you."

"But we've never gone out. Why don't we go to a hotel or a restaurant? One of them." She was screwing this up so much. "What about a witch dance?" Did they have those any longer?

He laughed. "Witch dance?"

It was a long shot and probably silly. "Never mind."

"They don't have them any longer," he said. "But we could go to the Carlton. They've got a nice restaurant there. I think I can still get in."

She toyed with the front of his shirt. "If you can, then let's go." She'd stepped out on a ledge, but she liked it. "I want to go out in public with you. Everyone sees us together."

"For the facade?" He nodded. "Right."

"No." She smoothed her palm over his chest. "For real."

"You're serious?"

She nodded. "I am."

He cleared his throat and eased his arm around her waist. "Lu?"

"I want to be with you. I'm clear-headed and know exactly what I want." She closed the gap between them, rubbing along his hip and chest. "You."

"You're sure?"

"Very." She held onto his shirt and brushed her lips over his. "Completely."

He groaned and tucked his hand into her back pocket, caressing her ass. "Fuck. I'm in. So in."

So was she.

* * *

A date? Holy shit. He couldn't remember the last time he'd been on a date. Not a real one. Thirty-four fucking years old and he didn't date.

"What?" She grinned. "You don't want to?"

"I want very much to." He kissed her temple. "When?"

"I don't know." She nuzzled his shoulder. "When do you want to go?"

"We've got work tonight, but I could leave." He caught his brother's gaze. When he needed a break, he and Lance had a signal. He tipped his head, then winked.

Lance grinned in return, then snapped his fingers, sending Court to the door.

"We now have the night off." Preston held onto her. "Ready?"

"I can't go until Denise shows up."

"She's here." Preston guided her to the kitchen. "She's been here for the last hour, but hanging out in the back. She'd rather get paid to stand around because it's easier than actually dealing with the public."

"Oh." She held onto him. "Lance is really okay with it?"

"I am." Lance rounded the prep counter. "I might have used magic to help, but you expected that."

Preston chuckled. "Thanks."

"Go and have a good time." Lance tossed his towel onto his shoulder, then left the kitchen.

"What was that?" she asked. "How?"

"When your brother owns the bar, you can do a lot and get away with even more."

"I guess so." She laughed and stayed beside him. "Now what?"

"We go out. I'm excited to be out with a beautiful woman." Beyond excited. He needed this chance.

"I'm glad. I should get my stuff."

He nodded. His belongings stayed on his person, and he'd forgotten she'd kept hers in the office. He waited as she tucked her apron into her bag, then donned her jacket. "Okay." She smiled. "Where do we go? Where's a safe place from the sorcerers?"

"There are lots of places." And nowhere, really. No place was good enough to take her, or safe from the sorcerers if they wanted to cause trouble. Still, he had to try. "We'll go to the apartment, then Conway's."

"Conway's?" The wattage of her smile increased. "I've never been there."

"Then it's time we go." He escorted her out to his car. "My dear." He opened the passenger door for her.

She settled on the seat. "Thank you."

He hurried around the hood to the driver's side and joined her in the car. His heart pounded. It'd been a long time since he'd been out on the town. He put the car into gear. "Ready?"

"For anything."

Her words spurred him on. He sped out of the lot and across the town to her apartment. Instead of stopping, they should head straight to the restaurant, but he smelled like the bar.

"Pres?"

"Yeah?" He turned into the parking garage. "What's wrong?"

"We were being followed."

"Shit." He turned behind the wall, blocking the view of the car. "What make and model?"

"Black sedan. Four doors. Not sure what make." She scrunched down in the seat. "Not sorcerers."

"Fuck me." He should've expected a problem. His father would go out of his way to make sure Preston didn't have a good evening. "We need to hide."

"No."

"No?" He sped through the garage to her parking spot. "Lu."

"We don't." She touched his arm. "I learned a spell that will give us cover."

"It will?" He'd love to hear this.

"Yes." She murmured something he couldn't make sense of, then pointed to him.

In an instant, his clothes changed. No more black tee and jeans. He wore a sport coat and button-down. When he glanced in the mirror, he noticed his hair was controlled and he swore he looked like he'd bathed, too. He didn't reek of fried food. He even wore dark jeans and polished cowboy boots.

"Good?" She beamed. "You could be a model."

"Not exactly." He held her hand, then kissed her knuckles. "Now do you."

She snorted. "That came out bad."

"It did." He kissed her knuckles again. "Do it."

"Pushy." She laughed, then murmured again. This time, she waved her hand over herself. Just as quickly as she'd changed him, she switched into a fresh outfit, too. The sundress contoured to her curves, and she smelled like flowers. The soft makeup accentuated her features and made his heart beat faster.

She stole his breath, and he swept his gaze over her again. "Wow."

"Good enough?" She blushed. "I'm not great at that spell."

"Not good?" She was fucking perfect. He slipped her hand into his. "I'm a lucky man to be out with you."

"I'm pretty lucky, too." She reached across the console and rested their clasped hands on his thigh.

"Babe." He'd never make it through the date. Not when he was already hard for her. Christ. Blood rushed to his dick and he swore he could drive nails into steel.

He did his best to focus on the road as he drove out of the garage. "Keep an eye out for the sedan." He sped across town, taking the scenic route. The faster he drove, the more he craved her. This wasn't mating magic. This was the real deal.

He pulled into the lot forty minutes later. Once he parked, he sucked in a ragged breath. She'd be the death of him, but he welcomed it. "Ready?"

"I am." She blushed again. "I've got to remember how to do this."

"Do what?"

"Date."

"You're fine."

"I have to remember how to be with someone who appreciates me."

"I do." He left the vehicle and hurried to her side of the car. He opened the door for her. "My love." Shit. He'd used the word love. Maybe she'd miss it.

"Thank you." She held his hand as she rose to her feet. She fell in step with him as he went into the restaurant.

A thought occurred to him in the foyer. He'd forgotten all about reservations.

"Welcome to Conway's." The hostess grinned. "Name?"

"Lance Hermes," Lulu said. "He called ahead."

"Two... Preston Hermes and Lulu Redwitch," Preston volunteered. He sure hoped his brother had come through for them.

"Yes." The hostess checked the book and tapped the page. "Yes, right here. Would you tell Mr. Hermes I said hello? He could call me. He never did."

Preston bit back a groan. Of course, Lance had done that. Lance loved to ghost people. "I will."

"He probably doesn't remember me. Sally Bortner? We had a great weekend, but that's all it was." She picked up two menus. "This way."

Preston angled Lu in front of him as they followed the hostess to the table. He'd have to thank his brother for the save, then give him shit for stringing Sally along.

"Right here. Tell Lance he owes me." The hostess placed the menus on the table. "Enjoy."

Preston pulled the chair out for Lulu before she perched on the seat. Once she settled, he sat across from her. "Get whatever you'd like." He barely spent money, so he had plenty and he'd spoil her rotten.

"Relax."

He hadn't realized his hands shook. "Sorry."

"I'm not going anywhere." She reached across the table and held onto his fingers. "I'm yours."

"You are?" He'd heard her, but he barely fathomed the strength of her words. He wasn't used to having someone.

"I am." She flicked her hair over her shoulder. "The candles are a nice touch."

He hadn't noticed the table decor. All he saw was her. "Brings out the sparkle in your eyes."

"Yeah?" She beamed again. "You're a lady killer."

"I'd rather make love to you." He hadn't meant to say that out loud or use the word love again, because it was too fast, but he had no regrets. He wanted to sleep with her right now.

"I do, too, but after something to eat that's not fried." She caressed his fingers. "Then we feast on each other."

Holy hell. "Yes." He so wanted that. More than his next breath.

Chapter Five

Lulu couldn't get into the car fast enough after dinner and a few dances. The food was great and the dancing even better, but she didn't want to be wrapped around him in public. She needed private time. "Drive."

"What do you think I'm doing?" He laughed. "I can't go any faster."

"You could." She reached across the console and smoothed her palm over his thigh up to his crotch. "We're not being followed and we've got all night, but I don't want to waste the rest of it in the car. Christ." The heat surged through her straight to her core. She massaged the bulge in his trousers.

"Like that?" He groaned. "Lu."

"Want me to stop?" She caressed a little harder. He sure seemed to be packing. She wanted to rip the clothes off him... right now.

He sped up the ramp to the parking spot in the garage. "I can't think straight and I'm not driving any better."

Her thoughts were a mess, too. "Yeah." She wished she could've allowed the date to last longer. Maybe a few more dances and held each other to delight in the atmosphere of the evening. She'd liked the music and food, but she needed him. He consumed her attention.

He parked and left the vehicle in a rush. She opened her door before he reached her side.

"You *are* excited." He closed the door behind her. "My dear."

She caged him in between her body and the car. "Can't wait." She mashed her mouth on his, drawing a gasp from within him.

He held tight to her hips, bunching her dress in his hands. He eased the hem up, brushing his fingers along her bare thighs. Higher and higher.

Any second now, she'd have her ass exposed to the parking garage. Did she care? No.

She groaned into the kiss. The magic overwhelmed her, but she wasn't afraid. She needed this.

He broke the kiss and panted. "We need to go inside. I don't share."

"Neither do I." She let go long enough to tug him into the building. She couldn't get into her apartment any faster. Despite her best efforts, she fumbled with her keys.

He kissed her shoulder. "Good girl. Slow down. We've got all night."

The commanding but soft tone of his voice kicked her desire up a notch, and she whipped around to face him.

He took control of the connection and pinned her to the door, then slipped the keys from her hand. He worked the lock, opening it. "Can't wait."

"Then don't." She ushered them into the apartment before slamming the door behind them.

She'd barely gotten a breath out when he pinned her to the door again, but this time inside the apartment. She crushed her mouth on his and at the same time, fumbled with his buckle as well as the button on his jeans.

He hiked her skirt up again, but this time, he didn't stop. He untied the strings on her panties, allowing the thin fabric to slip from her body.

A shiver ran the length of her spine as he tossed the panties out of sight. She managed to work his trousers open and down enough to free his dick. His shaft practically seared her hand. She stroked him. "I love it."

"Yeah?" He picked her up, off her feet and ground his shaft between the lips of her pussy. Her cream slicked the way. "Fuck, yes."

She held tightly to him, needing every ounce of him against her. She sucked on his tongue. The scent of him and heat from his body curled around her.

He said nothing as he entered her in one thrust. No finesse or time to think. Just right in. She wouldn't have this any other way. The frenetic pace pleased her. The push knocked the breath from her, and she broke the connection for a second. As she panted, she dug her nails into his shoulders. The scent of him enveloped her and his touch had her nerve endings on fire. "Pres."

"Babe." He kissed along her jaw to her throat. Within seconds, he built into a steady rhythm, pushing in deep before nearly pulling out.

Each push forced her against the door, but she craved the rough treatment. She curled her legs around his waist, giving him full access to her body. She gasped. The power of his body was more than she could handle, but she didn't want to miss a second. The orgasm built low in her belly, then spiraled through her body in an instant.

Nothing else mattered except him and this moment. She met him, as best she could, thrust for thrust.

"Fuck." He scraped his teeth along her throat. "Crave you."

She craved him, too. She wished she could tell him that, but the words were gone.

Sparkles and light surrounded her. She paused a second. This was new. Holy fuck. She'd never had sparkles show up during sex.

"Yes, babe." He pushed harder and moved deeper into her. "Mine."

"Yes." At least she could manage that. She clung to him. The sparkles increased and the light nearly blinded her. The orgasm overwhelmed her, and she squeezed her pussy tight around his shaft. The move held him tight within her body. A strangled cry escaped her throat.

"Yes, babe. Come for me." He pistoned into her. Each thrust stretched her to her limit. He marked her as he scraped his teeth along her bare skin again on her shoulder. He filled her to the hilt with his cock and she swore she'd never be the same.

"Come for me," he repeated. "Now. Come with me again."

Not that she could hold back. That was impossible, even after she'd just come. She cried out and every cell in her body screamed for him. She tensed, then relaxed as the climax hit.

"I love that." He slammed into her, then stilled. His cock throbbed within her. He kept her pressed to the door and rested his forehead on her shoulder. "Damn."

She dug her fingers into his biceps and her thoughts fizzled. The sparkles evaporated and the light faded.

"You blew my mind," he said. He carried her to the sofa. "Not sure how my knees are working to do this, but I'm glad they are." He placed her on the cushions, then collapsed beside her.

She swore her bones had melted. "You made me weak."

"Yeah?" He draped her legs over his and didn't bother to put his dick behind his zipper. "I like that."

She curled into his side. "I do, too." She stared at Preston. Until she'd come back to Eerie, she hadn't thought she'd find a partner, let alone love. When she looked at him, she didn't just see a lover or partner. He was so much more. Her other half? Possible.

She threaded her arm across his midsection. Sprawling together with him in a state of semi-undress felt oddly right. "Pres?"

"Yeah?" He kissed the top of her head. "What are you thinking about?"

Lots of things. "You."

"Me?" He chuckled.

She knew that sound -- his odd combination of nervousness and fear hidden under a laugh. "You."

"What about me?"

"Have you ever had sparkles appear during sex?" She arranged her legs across his and kicked off her flats.

"No. You?"

"Nope." She hoped he had so he could explain the phenomenon. "Never. I didn't know it was possible."

"It is, apparently. We did it." He caressed her shoulder. "Lu?"

"Right here." She toyed with the front of his shirt. "You've got something on your mind, don't you?"

"I do."

"What? Me?" She could only hope.

"I have a beautiful woman in my arms. I had hot sex with her, and the magic agreed. I should be on cloud nine."

That sounded almost perfect to her. "But?"

"I'm scared."

She paused. Scared? "Of? Me?"

"I'm afraid you'll see I'm still cursed, even after everything, and leave."

She hadn't missed the catch in his voice. He might look strong, but this was his weak point. He feared putting his heart on the line, especially because he could get it broken so easily. "Pres."

"I'm serious. My malady won't just go away because we had sex once."

She sat up and tipped his chin to force him to look her in the eye. "I don't let just anyone fuck me against a door. I don't let just *anyone* fuck me, for that matter." She'd never been so free with her body this way. "I don't bare my soul with anyone in the same way I have with you. I've never let my guard down or used my magic on someone, but I did the spell tonight so it'd be perfect."

"Has been so far," he said. "I'm sorry. Just gun-shy."

"I know." She caressed his cheek. "I'm scared, too, but the magic seems to know. It's guiding us. If it wasn't, then the sparkles, which must be part of it, wouldn't have materialized. Right?"

"Right."

She tugged on the front of his shirt. "Take me to bed. I want to make love there and create more sparkles. Our own kind of magic." She needed to. "No force or mating magic. Just the real thing that we created."

"True attraction?"

"Bone-deep." She kissed him hard on the lips. "Unbreakable." She knew to her soul she'd never be the same and didn't want to be. Not ever again. He flowed in the deepest parts of her. He was part of her. Now she had to prove to him he belonged there for good.

* * *

Preston panted and stared into her eyes. Holy fucking balls. He hadn't expected sex with her to be that explosive. Never thought he'd see that kind of magic, either. He should take her to the bedroom, but his legs refused to work.

"Preston?" She stood, then offered her hand. "I didn't mean for you to go caveman and carry me to the bedroom. Come on."

"Who says I didn't want to?" He stood, then scooped her into his arms. His pants tangled around his ankles and he managed to kick out of the wadded-up garments before making his way to the adjacent room.

She clung to him and laughed as he moved. "The cool air is making me shiver."

"On your bare pussy?" He kissed her. "I love that you're not wearing any underwear now."

"I love it, too." She blushed. "I've never been able to be this free with anyone before."

"No?" He liked the sound of that. He placed her on the bed, then promptly removed the rest of his clothing. He needed to be naked with her. No barriers. No lies. No one else between them -- even if she could see his curse.

She shrugged out of the dress before propping herself on her elbows before him. "Gonna fuck me now?"

"Such a dirty mouth." He crawled onto the bed and settled between her legs. "I should kiss you into surrender."

"You should."

The husky sound of her voice sent shivers down his spine. Blood rushed to his cock and his thoughts scattered. Every nerve ending tingled, and magic seemed to slide over his skin. The electricity in the room damn near overwhelmed him.

She reached for him. "Pres."

"Right here." He arranged her legs around his waist, then surged into her in one thrust. The second he came together with her, his world righted. Nothing else existed besides them. The tightness of her pussy, combined with the passion in her eyes, was more than he could handle.

"Pres." She arched beneath him and groaned. "I love it."

He hadn't done anything yet. He braced himself on his hocks and hands, then began to thrust. Slowly at first, giving himself time to build into a steady rhythm. He felt every ripple and nuance of her body. She squeezed around him, and his synapses misfired. He'd just come, but damn it, she had him right near the edge again.

"My God." She dug her heels into his lower back. "More."

He'd give her more. He bucked against her, pushing in as deep as possible before nearly pulling out. He never wanted this moment to end.

She moved with him, one body and one soul, in their own divine cadence. He sat back on his heels and tugged her closer until she straddled him. With his hands dug into her hips, he increased the speed of his thrusts. The sound of skin on skin and the whirl of magic filled the air.

"Oh, God." She shivered beneath him, then grasped his arms. She scratched his biceps. "Pres."

"Getting close?" He moved faster. "Gonna go over the edge?" He wasn't far from climax himself. The sheer delight of being with her and being free pleased him.

"I..." She slid her hands over her breasts, tweaking her nipples.

Seeing her pleasure herself while he fucked her turned his insides out. He couldn't think straight.

Sparkles and mist filled the air. Almost like being in the middle of a snow globe. He marveled at the sight. Their special magic created this effect. He'd never had anything like it before in his life. But he'd never had anyone like her in his life, either.

He'd given up on love. Given up on being with someone for more than a few days. Women saw him as a means to moving up. A stepping stone. Not her.

Until Lulu, he swore he'd be on his own for the remainder of his existence. The curse wouldn't be broken and he'd stay a satyr for the duration. Then she came along. Lulu changed everything. She made him feel. Made him think. Brought out his protective streak. Gave him a reason to keep going.

"Pres." She grasped his shoulders again. "I can't... I'm..." She shivered and tensed beneath him. When she moved, she held him tight in her body. The magic increased and the mist grew denser. She dug her nails hard into his skin.

He didn't feel a bit of the pain. All he experienced was pleasure.

"Come for me, Lu." He stared into her eyes. The connection to her overwhelmed him. He wasn't one for talking during sex. But this was so personal. So perfect. "Let go. I've got you. Scream, Lu."

She arched her back again and cried out. The vise-grip on his dick nudged him over the edge. As she came, he tumbled over with her. He surged deep into her and filled the woman he loved with his seed. The sparkles and mist filled the room, then dissipated in an instant. Like the magic was never there.

He collapsed onto his hands and curled over her. A fine sheen of perspiration… or was it magic and sparkles? He wasn't sure, but the glimmer on her skin added to her beauty. He'd fallen so hard for her. He'd never be the same.

Lulu panted. "Pres." A lazy smile curled on her lips. She draped her arms around his neck and sighed. "You wear me out."

"I don't." He nuzzled her throat. "It's the pleasure of being together."

"It overwhelms me." She lowered her legs but tugged him closer. "You make me happy."

"Same here." He licked and nipped at her throat. "My life has meaning when I'm with you." He'd never admitted that to anyone before.

"Pres." She slid her fingers through his hair. "I've never fallen for someone like you."

"No?" Someone like him? He wasn't sure how to take that.

"Not like you." She sighed. "Not at all."

"Lu?" He didn't want to push her but damn it. The words stung. She had no idea he wasn't confident or that he'd been burned so much. Not the full extent.

"Someone who cares about me, who wants to keep me safe, who sees me for me… I've never loved anyone like that until you." She tipped his head. "You're original. I can't imagine doing this without you."

She'd touched him in ways he never thought could be breached. He stared at her. The sparkles were gone, but the smile was brighter than ever. She truly cared about him.

"What?" she whispered. She toyed with his hair again. "You're lost in thought."

"Lost in your eyes." He nuzzled her cheek. "You

entrance me."

"I do?"

The shock in her voice amused him. Such an innocent, despite the abuse and horror she'd seen. "Yes, you do."

Her grin faded.

"Now you're lost in thought." He pulled out and rolled off her, settling beside her on the bed. "What's wrong?"

"Nothing." She averted her gaze. "It's nothing."

"Is it me?" He propped himself on his side and slid his hand over her belly. He laced his fingers with hers. "Talk to me." She had to be realizing he was a fucking satyr. She must be having second thoughts. She'd confessed so much, but the good things in his life tended to go to shit.

Her chin quivered and she blinked back tears.

Here it comes, he thought. *The rejection.* He fought the urge to speak and instead kept his mouth shut. She didn't need the encouragement to dump him. He looked like a fucking monster and freak. Hairy legs. Hooves. Fucking fuck.

A tear slipped down her cheek.

"Lu?" He couldn't handle seeing her cry. He'd always been a softie when it came to women crying. "Talk to me." Had his father infiltrated her mind? He wished he understood.

"I'm scared," she murmured.

"Of what? Me?" He hoped not.

"No." She faced him and twined their legs. "I'm scared this won't last. I know down to my bones that you're the one I want. You're the one I never saw coming and the one I need in my life. I can't do this without you, like I said."

"But?"

She sighed. "I don't know how to say this."

"I'm a satyr and you're turned-off? You got what you wanted and you're done?" The words tumbled out faster than he could keep them at bay. Damn it.

"No." She frowned, then a smile curled at the corners of her mouth. "Not that at all."

"No?" Seriously? He'd always been plagued with the curse.

"I don't care what you look like." She traced a shape over his heart. "This is what I care about. This right here. Your heart."

She'd caught him speechless. His heart. She cared about his heart?

"I know this is mine. Just like my heart is yours." She ran her fingers over his chest again. "But I'm afraid. You're the one I want, but I'm scared you'll be taken from me."

"You're the one who could be taken." If his father caught wind of the situation.

"I know, but that doesn't worry me. No one wants me that badly. My ex maybe. Those stupid sorcerers, I'm sure. But the one I'm scared of is the one who will take you from me."

"No one's going to take me." No one else wanted him. He'd sworn he'd die alone.

"The magic we created is something I've never seen. Never experienced. It's true and powerful." She slid her palm over his cheek. "And it's scary because the wrong people will want to use it. The sorcerers, among others."

"They'll have to go through me." He'd make that extremely clear.

"I know and that's what scares me. I finally found you and you'll be taken from me because you'll try to defend me. It's not right." Her voice cracked.

"I've waited for so long for someone to balance me. Be my other half. Understand me. Then you come along and you're nothing like I expected which is why you're perfect."

"No one will take me from you." He'd make damn sure of it.

"You can't promise me that." She shook her head. "No magic is strong enough to bring someone back from the dead."

"No, but love and devotion are strong enough to bring me back to you. I've taken a lot of shit in my day. I can take more if it means keeping you. I'll do whatever's required."

"Pres."

She didn't believe him. He nodded once. "Satyrs are odd beings. We're here to lure and create merriment, but we're also ridiculously loyal. We're also damn stubborn. We know what we want and don't take no for an answer. I'll give my life for you, but whoever wants that is going to have to pay dearly. I don't roll over that fast when something so precious is in my grasp."

"I'm precious?"

"You are." The most precious thing he'd ever touched.

"Stay with me tonight."

He did every night. "I will."

"No." She petted his hair. "Right here. Beside me under the covers. I don't want this night to end."

"It won't." He shifted enough to cover them with the blankets, then settled down with her in his arms. He'd never let her go. Not without a fight. He'd created magic he didn't understand with the woman he'd never expected to meet.

Hope blossomed in his heart. She might be the

one to break his curse. If she could love him back, then he'd be set. He already loved her. If fate and the magic kept going his way, he'd be trapped in her silken bonds and free forever. Best place he could imagine.

But right now, it was just a dream.

At least he could dream about the curse being broken and hold onto his faith. The magic was at the helm and all he could do was hold on tight for the ride. She mattered. He'd give his all for her. No matter what.

Chapter Six

The next morning, Lulu woke before Preston. She slipped from bed and let him sleep. Once she donned a robe, she padded silently to the living room to think. She'd slept plenty the night before, but the course of events played heavily in her mind.

The date had been the best night of her life. Lance had been right -- once she got Preston away from the bar, he shone. Hell, he was incandescent. She'd never seen him so happy. Then again, she hadn't known him that long. Working at the bar only showed her some parts of him. He wasn't able to be the full version of himself.

She curled up in the armchair and tucked her knees to her chest. Too many things he'd said, though, bothered her. Not that he cared about her. That'd made her day. It made her life. Not that he'd fallen for her. She'd felt that from the moment they'd met. No, it was his continual mention of the satyr thing. His physical appearance didn't matter to her. His heart did. Did he see that? No. He fixated on that form. She sighed. One day he'd see himself the way she saw him. A sexy, handsome man. One day.

She toyed with the hem of the robe. The thing about his father stealing her still bothered her, too. He hadn't mentioned it, but she could see the worry in his eyes. She wasn't going anywhere. Not to his father -- whoever the fucker was -- or anyone else. But why did he think she'd just wander off with the God? Because he was a God? Big fucking deal.

Still, she couldn't help her fear that things would fall apart. Not that he'd leave her. He wasn't that type. She worried the sorcerer would step in and kill Preston. Or her ex would come back. She shivered.

Reuben wasn't around, but she could feel his presence. He'd never let her go. Wasn't his style. She could run. Could even hide a while. But he'd find her.

Another presence slid into her mind. She didn't know this person. A vision of a man came into focus. A younger-looking man, easy on the eyes, but forthright. He flicked his hand, then appeared before her in the flesh. She gasped, but wasn't entirely surprised by the show of magic. She'd grown up in Eerie and beings appearing and disappearing this way wasn't out of the ordinary. Still, she kept up her guard and balled her hand. One scream and she'd have Preston out there in a second.

"Yes?" she asked. "Why are you in my space?" She didn't detect sorcerer from him. No, not even much magic. More like power.

He winked. "You're involved with Preston."

"I am." She kept her hands tight in fists. "So?"

"You know his reputation."

What an ass. "I do."

"And you're still with him?"

Her assessment of the man wasn't wrong. "I am."

"You know he's cursed."

"I do." She narrowed her eyes. "Who are you?"

The man tipped his head back slightly and squared his shoulders. "I'm Hermes."

"Okay?" She knew the name and legend, but wasn't impressed.

"You know who I am." He leveled his gaze at her. "A God."

"So what?" She wasn't interested in him. "Why are you here?"

"You know his job, yes?" Hermes folded his arms. "To bring me lovers. He should've delivered you by now. What's the wait?"

"Hold up." She rolled her eyes. "There isn't a wait. I don't want to be your lover. I don't want to know you. You're not my type and I don't want to be with a God, no matter how high or low you are."

"You don't?" He curled his lip in a sneer. "You're to be with me."

"I don't get a say in this?" She shook her head. "Sorry. Go bother someone else. I'm not interested." She left the chair and matched his stance.

"I have misheard you," he snapped. "You're coming with me."

"The hell I am." She wasn't dressed to go anywhere, and she refused to leave with this bastard. "Get out of my apartment."

"You cannot order a God around." He reached for her, but she darted out of the way. She sprinted into the bedroom. "Pres." She jostled him, but he didn't move. Not a bit. What the hell? She pushed on him, expecting a response, but got nothing.

"He sleeps." Hermes stood beside her. "He won't move while I'm here. He can't."

"Why the fuck not?" She faced the god but continued to nudge Preston. "What's wrong with him?"

"Besides being a satyr?" Hermes grasped her bicep. "He's incapable of preventing me from taking you. You're here for my pleasure. He can test the goods, but he can't keep them."

Test the goods? Like she was an object. What nerve! She tried to yank free from him, but he held firm. "Let. Go." She gritted her teeth and tried to get loose. "Now."

"You can fight, but you're not going to win. You won't. I'm a God and you're simply a witch." The muscle in Hermes' jaw fluttered. "Now, let's go." He pulled hard on her and the room turned black.

Wind rushed past her and her stomach churned. She tried not to cling to Hermes, but she swore she'd be sick. "Where are you taking me?"

"Olympus. Hasn't he told you anything?" Hermes stopped moving and the space around him cleared. A mountain retreat came into view. "You will live here and be at my beck and call. You will be one of my lovers and tend to me. If you choose not to, you'll be thrown in prison. Understand?"

She understood all too well. When she looked out the window, she saw the tops of the clouds and the mountain. The marble and wood palace stretched out before her. She gasped at the lush furs on the walls and the shimmering columns. A gaggle of women stood off to the side, dressed in gauzy outfits that barely contained their assets. She planted her feet. If she could've picked this place to live with Preston, she might have jumped at the offer. But he wasn't permitted there, and she wasn't sure how to escape. She refused to be yet another conquest for the God.

"What happened to Preston?" She faced Hermes as he let her go. "Why couldn't he move?"

"Simple. He's there to work for me and I didn't need him, so he's incapacitated." Hermes nudged her forward. "Get changed. I expect you at the next orgy."

"The hell I will." She held up her hands and looked for anywhere to run.

"Grab her." Hermes flicked his fingers. "Guards! I hate when they're non-compliant. Get her out of here. If she won't be my lover, then she can rot in the prison."

Before she could get her bearings, two guards grabbed her in an iron grip. She shivered with anger and fear. How dare he kidnap her, then throw her in jail because she wasn't going to sleep with him! He wasn't a God. He was a monster.

The men yanked her, shoving her around as they dragged her from the room. Hermes laughed and the sound echoed in her mind. Not a fun laugh. Maniacal.

She tensed in their grip. The space switched from fancy marble and thick rugs to dusty, dirty limestone. Water dripped from the walls and the stench of decay hung in the air. The stone chafed at her bare feet. She struggled, despite knowing she had no choice but to go with them.

The sounds of screams rang out. She wanted to run away, but where would she go? Call out for Preston? At this rate, he was probably frozen again. Maybe hadn't been unfrozen yet. The darkness of the space surrounded her.

"If you'd only be a good girl, you'd get whatever you want." One of the guards tossed her forward, while the other held on. He laughed. "You could've been the mistress of a god. Now you're just another prisoner."

"Watch for the rats. They fight back," the second guard said. He let go and shoved her into the cell. "Don't bother to scream. No one cares. No one will release you."

She collided with the wall and grunted. The scrape of the wall tore at her robe. At least she was still covered. She drank in the view of her new cell. Crumbling walls, water sliding down the surface. A suspect stain on the floor. Nowhere to sit and just a hole in the ground. Barbaric.

She rubbed her arms, careful of the tenderness from the guards' manhandling her. Their words stuck in her mind. No one cared. No one would release her.

"Preston," she murmured. "I don't know if you can hear me. Don't know if you're frozen, but you've got to help me. Please listen for me."

Panic and fear filled her brain. The urge to run crossed her mind. She rubbed her hands on her thighs and fought the urge to grasp the bars. Could be dirty or even poisoned. She'd never heard of anyone being imprisoned on Olympus, but it had to be possible -- she'd been tossed in jail.

She trembled. Reuben had been terrible, but this was worse. She paced the length of the space. She had to get out of here. Had to. But how? No windows. One door -- the bars. The thick lock dangled from the handle.

If only Preston could help her, he'd save her. She had no doubt. He'd be pissed when given the ability to move again. Confused, too. She paused. Maybe not. He might know exactly what was going to happen. Realization dawned on her. He'd been trying to warn her the entire time. Not that his father would take her, but that he'd protect her. He'd sealed himself to her. He'd heard her before. It was possible he could hear her again.

"Preston," she murmured. "I'm in trouble. He got me. Please help me, if you can hear me. Please. I need you."

She'd used her wits to get the hell away from Reuben, but this was bigger than her ex. This was magic and a god. She had to trust that fate and faith wanted her to be with Preston and that he'd be okay. He'd find her. He'd save her. But until he did, she'd do her dead level best to save herself first. No man, spirit, magical being or even god had the right to own her. No one had the right to kidnap her. Her life was hers and they could fuck themselves.

* * *

Preston screamed, despite the lack of sound. Frozen. God damn it. He'd had the feeling his father would pull this shit. He'd finally grown close to someone. Not just anyone. Lulu. She was one in a million. She'd seen past his curse and fallen for him. Sure, she hadn't said she loved him, but damn it, the feeling was there.

He tensed. He could hear the sounds of her fear -- the shrieking, the whimpering. The scrape of her feet on the floor and the whoosh of the magic taking her from the room.

He couldn't speak. Couldn't fight back. That was what his father wanted. The less resistance, the better. If she didn't resist, she'd be part of the chorus of lovers. If she did fight back or turn him down, she'd be imprisoned.

He'd felt her hands on his body. The shaking, the panic, the immediacy. He couldn't help her. Not yet.

Being frozen in place and unable to fight back was part of the curse. She had to resist his father, but she also had to tell him she loved him to help reverse his problem. To make him anything but a fucking satyr. But she couldn't say anything when she wasn't there. He gritted his teeth. She'd been kidnapped, and he couldn't do a damn thing yet.

He growled to himself and used every ounce of his energy to fight against the curse. Anything to get free. His growl split the air as he managed to sit up. He bounced off the bed to his feet. His heart hammered. *Free!* Now what to do?

He dressed in a pair of boxer shorts, then checked the room for signs of her being there or where she'd gone. He had a pretty good idea, but she could've left some clues.

Preston scrubbed his hand over his mouth. The magic should've been enough. No matter how hard he looked around the room, he saw nothing. His father had been cutthroat this time. No clues. Nothing.

Shit. He rested his hands on his hips. If Hermes took her anywhere, it'd be Olympus to be part of his bevy of women. If she truly cared about him and didn't want anything to do with Hermes, she'd be imprisoned. He'd have to break her out. He sighed. But he couldn't do it alone. If anyone could help him, it was his brother. Lance could be a pain in his ass, but at least he'd try.

He strode out to the living room and located his phone. Within seconds, he dialed his brother's number.

The panic and fear in Lulu's voice resonated in his head. He'd never be able to silence the sound. Never. It'd be a scar on his soul for the duration.

After three rings, his brother answered. "Where are you?" Lance asked. "You left, which I don't care about, but you're usually good for letting me know where you are."

Such was life with a brother. If nothing else, Lance cared. "I'm at Lulu's place."

"She's safe?"

"No." He pinched the bridge of his nose and paced. "Our father struck."

"Fuck," Lance whispered. "When?"

"Within the hour. I couldn't do anything. Just lie there frozen." He shook his head. "I was so useless."

"That's the curse. It's not your fault," Lance said. "What do you need from me?"

"Help busting her out."

Lance snorted. "You're sure she's been imprisoned? Not giving in?"

"I know her. She's a romantic, but not like that.

Dear Old Dad is a piece of work and scares her. She wouldn't submit to him in any fashion." He knew that to his core. "She's got to be in prison."

"Our father is an ass."

"Agreed." But calling Hermes names wasn't going to help Lulu. "I need to get her out, and you've got to help me." They needed a plan.

"Okay. How?"

"You know more people than I do." Lance was the schmoozer. Preston was considered the user. Preston stopped pacing. "Can we get help from the queen?" He'd never considered asking, but this was a problem bigger than even he and Lance could handle.

"Wow. I don't know." Lance paused. "You think she'd be the only one to convince Hermes to let Lulu go?"

"She's got to be. He won't listen to you and disregards me. I'm nothing." He shuddered at the memory of the last time he'd argued with his father. He'd tried to keep Analise from being taken and Hermes simply used magic to paralyze him. Analise walked off, never to be seen again. He couldn't handle seeing the same thing happen to Lulu.

"Give me half an hour. If you can, come to the bar and I'll get in touch with the queen. If we're lucky, she'll reply." Lance hung up.

No chance for a reply. Just silence. He tossed the phone onto the couch and retrieved his clothes. If he had any chance to helping Lulu and bringing her home, then he needed more than just his fucking underwear.

He dressed in record time, then collected his phone, wallet and keys, and left the apartment. Despite the fact he had no wings, he practically flew to the bar. He had to pray no police would find him. This was bigger than a damn speeding ticket in her car.

When he pulled into the lot behind the bar, Lance stood at the back door. He surged forward and opened the passenger door. "She's waiting on us at the palace," Lance said. "I don't know how she knew we needed her, but she answered right away."

"Not a crank?" Preston waited for his brother to settle into his seat before he peeled out of the lot. He'd never been to the palace. Would they even allow him onto the property?

"Nope. The real queen." Lance buckled his belt. "I thought it might be a lie, too, but the Cyclops spoke to me, too."

"Diesel?" Holy shit.

"The one and only."

"How do you know him?" He hadn't realized Lance knew the king consort.

"He'd come into the bar when you weren't there. Not because you weren't there, but during that year you left for school. I always wanted you to meet him because he's a fascinating guy, but then he stopped coming in." Lance shrugged. "I guess he pulled into himself and started working with his sister at the hotel. I don't know. I never understood why he hid. He's got that dangerous sexy thing going on."

If he didn't know his brother so well, he'd think Lance was babbling. No, this was Lance's way of filling the silence and not focusing on the tension.

"We need a plan." He drove across town to the gates of the palace. "Do we need some sort of special word to get in? A code?"

"The gates are open, remember? The queen wanted the place to be accessible to everyone." Lance pointed to the entrance. "But if we're asked, we're here to see the queen and have the Cyclops' permission."

"Right." He had to hope this would work. Jesus H. Christ. He stopped at the gate and sucked in a ragged breath. Things could go sideways, or they could go well. He had to hope for the best.

The guard stepped out from behind the glass and pointed to them. "You have business here, satyr? Lance."

Preston nodded. He hated being a satyr, but today was the worst day. He flexed his hands on the steering wheel. "I do. I'm here to see the queen with the permission of the Cyclops."

"Lance?" The guard leaned over, peering at Lance. "Is that true?"

"Why else would we be here?" Lance asked. "I know well enough to stay off this property without reason."

He did? Preston forced himself to remain calm. He'd ask Lance about that later.

"I see." The guard fiddled with his phone, then waved his fingers. "It appears you're telling the truth, but know I have my eyes on you. One foot out of line and you'll be in the dungeon, do you understand?"

Preston tensed. He hadn't planned on acting out. He needed help. "Understood."

"Hades, you won't let that one prank die, will you, Gus?" Lance shook his head. "No, I won't step out of line. It was a prank fifteen years ago and a stupid one at that. I've matured a bit. I know how to behave."

"Just show you do." The guard opened the gate, allowing them through.

Preston nodded to thank him, then drove away. He relaxed his hands on the wheel. "What was that about?"

"When we didn't have a king, I may have egged the gates." Lance folded his arms. "I was a kid.

Seventeen? Something like that. It seemed like a good thing at the time because I was pissed that we weren't respecting the rules."

"You hate rules."

"I do, but I hated that the people in charge were destroying so much of the castle. Like the royals and our heritage never existed. Pissed me off." Lance shrugged. "So I egged the gates and was escorted off the property by that guard, Gus. He won't forget what I did."

"He's afraid you'll do it again."

"He is." Lance unfolded himself and pointed to the spots where two other cars were parked. "There. We're expected inside within the hour."

His pulse sped up and he gritted his teeth again. He could do this. If he wanted to save Lulu, he had to meet with the powerful beings who could help him. If nothing else, the queen was his best hope.

He could do this.

Chapter Seven

Lulu stood in the middle of the cell until her legs wouldn't hold her any longer. She didn't want to sit on the ground, not without panties, but she'd had little choice. She chided herself. Normally, she slept with some kind of clothing on. Color inside the lines, behave, cover up, stay under control... Sleeping nude with Preston wasn't her norm, but she didn't have any regrets. She hadn't taken the time to conjure something else to sleep in.

"Who's there?"

She froze. She hadn't known anyone else was in the prison with her. "Sorry?"

"Who's there?" the voice asked again.

She strained to listen. The speaker sounded female, but she wasn't sure. "Who's there?" she repeated. "I'm not alone?"

"No. Across the way!" A figure came into slight focus. "You're here?"

"I am. Who are you?" She crept up to the bars, careful not to touch them. "How did you get down here?"

The figure clutched the bars. In the dim light, her features came into focus. Sad eyes, gaunt frame, pale skin. She flexed her thin fingers. "I didn't know anyone else would be thrown down here."

"I was. Who are you?" She stared, drinking in the view of the other woman.

"Analise." She sighed. "I thought I wanted to be with a god, then I got the chance and it wasn't what I expected. I was just another piece of meat. Not valued."

"I'm sorry." She swore she knew that voice. Preston had mentioned a former girlfriend named

Analise. Was this the same one? "You were rejected?"

"I rejected him, first." Analise shook her head. "You'll never get out of here. He doesn't waver."

"I didn't think he would." She hated what was happening, even if she appeared to be making a friend. "You wanted to be part of the group? The girls?"

"Originally, I thought I could be enough to make him change his mind. Be with just me. What a fool. He never wanted one of us. Always a group. He needs the fawning and I don't want that. I want one man."

"One satyr?" She'd asked a dangerous question, but she had to know the truth.

"Preston?" Analise's voice grew soft. "I was so terrible to him. I thought I could love him, but how can anyone love a man with hooves? I can't. It was so strange."

"He's a good man." Different, but good. "He tries."

"He tries to get into the pants of every woman he runs into so he can shove them off to his father. He's a louse."

"But you were with him. You didn't have feelings for him?" She'd rather be trying to figure out how to get the hell out of the cell, but Analise wanted to talk, so they would. "We can't get out of here? Can't bribe anyone?"

"Nope. The guards don't care. They're loyal to him. They want him to have all the women, too, because they take from them sometimes." She shook her head. "You'll be recruited, you know."

"I doubt that." She'd been too much of a troublemaker. "I want out. I don't belong here."

"I'm sorry for that. You're stuck here," Analise said. "No one will hear us scream or come for us."

"You don't think so?" She had to believe so.

"I've been here for three years, and Preston never bothered," Analise said. "He said he loved me and he'd never leave, but he left me here."

"You sort of left him first." She finally settled on the floor. "I'm sorry, too. I bet you had a good connection with him."

"He's a satyr. He flirts with everyone and ignored me. We had a relationship, but it could've been so much better if he'd been normal."

Lulu shook her head. "Normal isn't always what it's cracked up to be." She stared at Analise. "What's your power?"

"Huh?"

"You're in Eerie, so you have a power. You're para," Lulu said. "What's your power?"

"Since I've been in here, no one's asked me." Analise held onto the bars again. "I'm an elf. I make things. Doesn't help much when you're locked up. I don't have access to the things needed to create with."

"That's okay." She'd asked simply to make conversation. She noticed the guards at the end of the corridor sleeping. So much for being loyal. Or maybe they were sleep-deprived and finally collapsed. But if they could sleep, then maybe she could help them sleep and use her magic to get out.

"It's so unfair. We're wasted down here. We could be creating clothing for him or cooking or whatever. But because we don't want to sleep with him, we're locked up," Analise said. "It's not right."

"No." She stood and eyeballed the guards again. Her magic wasn't great, but if she summoned the power of love and desire she'd used with Preston, it might help her create the right amount of force to bust through the bars. She'd create a commotion, too, and wasn't sure how to navigate the corridors, but there had to be a way. Something had to work.

"What are you thinking?" Analise asked. "You're quiet."

"I'm listening." It wasn't a lie. The cadence of the snores grew even, and the sound of voices was softer. She didn't have much time.

"To me? That's a laugh. No one listens to me. The guards even tell me to shut up," Analise said. "They think I talk too much."

Good. She'd be a decent distraction, then. Lulu moved from the bars and out of Analise's sight so she could summon her magic.

"Preston," she murmured, "if you've got any power to lend me, I could use it. I'm coming home." She flicked her fingers and turned her thoughts to Preston, the love they shared and the future she wanted. She'd never focused on anyone but the men she'd been with. It was time to focus on herself, too. What did she want? Who did she want?

Preston. A future with him. A future of freedom. She drew in a deep breath and flexed her fingers.

"I wouldn't do that if I were you."

She snapped her eyes open and froze. She knew that voice. Reuben.

He stepped into the cell, moving right through the bars. Of course he did. He was a damn sorcerer. The suit fit him well and accentuated his muscled frame. He kept his hands behind his back and his shoes glittered as he walked around her.

"I see you're not above being sexy to bribe the guards." Reuben narrowed his eyes. "Always a game with you. Always an angle."

"Who said that?" Her blood chilled. She could feel the fingers of his mental control filling her brain. Fuck him. He wasn't allowed to have that control any longer. She squared her shoulders. "I might be the same girl you knew, but I'm not in the same shape."

"I can tell. You're thinner." He swept his gaze over her. "You smell of satyr."

"You slept with Preston?" Analise shouted. "I knew it. You were too nice concerning him."

For the love of Hades. She forced herself to remain composed. She couldn't argue with Analise and hold off Reuben at the same time.

Reuben crooked his brow. "So you didn't fall for the mighty God. That's good. You're not meant for him. Your magic is too... original." He tipped his head, then curled his fingers under her chin. "You're still beautiful and your magic is beyond compare. You simply need someone to take the reins. You slipped my grasp once, but you're not going to again."

She glared at him. "How did you get in here? The guards won't let anyone out. Hermes put me here because I wasn't cooperating. Do you know him? Have a line on how to get in and out?" If he did, she'd use his ass to get the fuck out.

"I'm a sorcerer. I can do many things no one else can." Reuben caressed her chin with the pad of his thumb. "Now, about getting you out."

"Yes." She resisted his attempts to infiltrate her mind. He wasn't going to win this time. She'd slipped his chain before, and she'd do it now.

"It's about time you were agreeable." Reuben continued to caress her chin. "Now, fork over the magic and control. You know you need to be controlled."

"Do I?" She hadn't wanted him to control her in the first place. She focused on her anger and hatred toward him. He'd done so much to ruin her life. Her skin sizzled and electricity crackled within her. She'd felt this powerful before, but only with Preston. She needed all the strength he could give her and all the gumption she possessed within herself.

"Girl." Reuben's gaze turned cold. He curled his lip in a sneer. "You have one job. Do it."

She did. She drew in a deep breath, then unleashed the power. A shimmer of light, something akin to a nuclear blast thundered through the cell. Reuben's eyes widened, then bugged out of his head as he vibrated. He opened his mouth, but no sound came out. Instead, he wobbled, then evaporated before her. Within seconds, nothing but a puff of smoke.

The walls rumbled and soot slipped down to the ground. The bars melted, allowing her access to the corridor. She peeked out into the vastness of the hallway. Analise joined her.

"What are you?" Analise wrapped her arms around herself. "I didn't know anyone could melt metal. You're dangerous."

"You have no idea. Let's get the fuck out of here." She swatted at Analise. She wasn't about to waste any more time. Hermes and Reuben could fuck off. She deserved to be free.

* * *

Preston flattened his hands on his thighs as he walked into the throne room. He'd never been into the castle, much less the fanciest room. He hated being here. There was too much expense and luxury. He didn't belong in such a fancy environment.

A voice filled his mind.

"*Preston.*" He knew that voice. Lulu.

She didn't sound panicked. Instead, she sounded strong. He tipped his head. Where was she? He elbowed his brother.

"Pres." Lance stood tall and clutched his hands

behind his back. "We're in public."

"I can hear Lu." He elbowed Lance again. "She sounds different."

"Does she?" Lance stared at him. "How? Think she got free? Or she capitulated."

"No." He listened for her again. Her voice came through like it was on a loop. He needed more. "I can't find her." He wasn't sure where she'd gone.

"Is she fainter?" Lance asked. "No?"

"I can't tell." His heart squeezed. He should be saving her, not listening for her. "I have to go."

"Where? You don't even know where she is." Lance's eyes widened. "I think I hear them coming."

Shit. He matched Lance's position and stood tall. The queen and Cyclops came into the room. He wasn't sure what he'd expected from the queen, but the beautiful yet approachable woman before him wasn't it. She smiled and rushed right up to him.

"You must be Preston." The queen held out her hand. "I'm Piper. It's nice to meet you."

"I -- thank you?" Was that the right thing to say to the queen? Had he spoken out of turn? Shit, shit, shit. "I'm sorry."

"You're fine." Piper chuckled. "I hear you need my help." She folded her arms after he shook hands with her.

"We do," Lance said. "His partner is missing."

"You must be Lance." She grinned again. "It's wonderful to meet you. I've told Diesel we need to get to your bar one of these days. It's not good to have an establishment and not visit it. We will."

"I… yes." Lance nodded. "Thank you."

Preston snorted. If the queen and Cyclops walked together into the bar, most of the patrons would pass out or think it was a raid. "Thank you for your help."

"You don't even know what I'm going to do yet." She snapped her fingers. "Diesel?"

The Cyclops stepped forward. "We have eyes on the woman, and she's escaped. She's loose."

"Loose?" Preston's heart skipped a beat. She'd gotten away? "Where is she?"

"We can't be certain, but she's not under the influence of the god," Diesel said. "I've got sentinels out there to intercept her, but it's going to be hard to convince her to go with them. She's scared."

"No kidding." Preston flexed his hands. "Okay, so what do we do? Can you take me to her?" He had to get to Lulu.

"We can." Diesel put his hands up. "Slow down. You're ready to run, but you can't. She's not ready. We have to get her mind cleared."

"You're going to do what?" Mind cleared? What if she forgot about him? "Is that a good idea?" He'd been too bold, but he didn't care. He had to protect Lulu.

Piper stepped between him and Lance. "First, you need to focus. We've got her. She's going to be safe. Yes?"

The way she met his gaze and stared at him, he had no choice but to listen. "Okay." He wasn't convinced of the plan, but he'd cooperate.

"Second, I've got damn scary magic. Reuben and Hermes don't want to argue with me," Piper said. "They can try, though."

He hesitated. He knew full well she had strong magic. She was the queen and it was expected, but he didn't know her.

"Third, you're scared. You need to calm down and breathe. We don't want to see harm come to you, satyr. You're a special man in our town." She smiled. "You know how to read people. You're smart and have a good heart. Just like your brother, you're a good man."

Lance's eyes widened. "You know me?"

"I've kept an eye on both of you." Piper stepped back. "Diesel?"

"We have her in our custody." Diesel brought over an orb. He held the shiny ball in his hand. A vision of Lulu filled the space and rubbed her arms. She wore a pink robe, but had dirt all over her face. She had another woman with her.

Preston stared at the image. Seeing Lulu safe, but filthy, both annoyed and pleased him. He hated to see her upset or sullied, but he appreciated knowing she was safe.

"Who's with him?" Lance leaned in close. "Isn't that Analise? Holy shit."

His breath clogged in his throat. Analise? He'd thought she was gone forever. A lover of Hermes. He stared at her. He'd once thought he loved her. Thought she might be his forever. Now when he looked at her, he wasn't so sure. His heart beat for Lulu. He needed to save her. But Analise?

"They're being brought here shortly." Diesel tossed the globe into the air where it disappeared. "Ready yourselves for the reunification."

Preston wobbled. Reunification? With Analise, too? "How fast?"

"A few moments." Diesel left the room.

Piper remained with Preston and Lance. "You seem uneasy?" she asked. "What's wrong? I can see your heart and you want Lulu back."

"I do." But he wasn't sure he could handle seeing Analise. He'd fallen out of love with her in her absence.

Her desertion of him hadn't helped.

"Pres?" Lance tipped his head. "What's wrong? It's her, isn't it?"

His brother, unfortunately, knew him well. "It is."

Piper's brow crinkled. "You used to love the other woman." She touched his arm. "I can see your heart, you know."

"I know." He feared what she could see.

"It's pure and full of love for Lulu," she said. "Analise will understand."

"Are you sure?" Lance asked. "She used to be his intended."

He wanted to kick his brother and his big mouth. "Lance…"

"I know," Piper said. She gestured to someone behind Preston. "Lance? Will you help Diesel?"

"Yes, ma'am." Lance bowed, then left the room.

Piper turned her attention back to Preston. "You don't trust me?"

"It's not that." He hesitated again. He needed to tell the queen the truth. If nothing else, it'd set him free. "I used to love Analise. I thought she'd be the one to break my curse, but she went for my father. I never heard from her again, and now that I see there was a jail situation involved, I wonder if she wanted to find me but couldn't. I'm afraid I might have made a mistake in letting go so easily." It hadn't been easy, but everything was so fucked up.

"You let go of her?" Piper gestured to a small, tufted bench. "Sit."

He complied. "I did."

"You're cursed, yes?" Piper folded her hands on her lap. "That's why you're a satyr."

"Yes." He bit back a groan. Fuck. "I am."

"Because your father is terrible. He knew better than to curse his own son," she said. "I know why he did."

The blood seemed to drain from his face. He wobbled. He'd never heard why he'd been cursed. Just excuses. "Why?"

"Your father knew you and Lance were more vivacious and intriguing than him. He's a god, but he's not that fantastic. Not really. He was jealous of you and your brother." She tipped her head. "It's the truth."

"Why just curse me? What was Lance's curse?" He hated asking that.

"Lance is cursed with his looks, but also with the lack of commitment. Ever noticed how he can't seem to snag a girlfriend for all that long? He's charismatic, but can't seem to keep anyone around."

He'd noticed, but thought his brother was a player.

"He's cursed to be single, but attractive. He probably doesn't even realize it. You, other the other hand, was the one who got the more obvious curse. Your father fears you." She crooked her brow. "He knows you're capable of being loved and loving someone. You've shown that multiple times."

"But which one do I choose? I loved Analise until I thought she'd chosen my father. I love Lulu, but what if I was supposed to be with Analise?" His stomach churned. "What if I pick the wrong one?"

"You won't." She smiled. "You'll know when you see them. You will."

He almost asked if she was sure, but kept his mouth shut. She was the queen and had powerful magic. If she said he'd understand and know, then he would.

"Believe in the power of your connections and that the curse will be lifted. You'll see." She winked. "Besides, they're here."

His breath lodged in his throat. The girls were both here? He'd have to face the woman he loved and the woman he'd once thought he loved. He'd have to make a decision. Choose one and leave the other behind. He wasn't even sure he could do it. He'd loved Analise, but he didn't know her. He loved Lulu, but she might not want a satyr. He'd be alone. Again.

Fucking shit.

Chapter Eight

Lulu tugged the thin robe tighter around her body. She hated not having more to wear and she wasn't a fan of the questions the Cyclops kept asking her. She didn't know him, so why did he want to know about her past? If Preston would've been there, he would've seen right through the smoke. But he wasn't here.

She rubbed her arms again. "Can I at least have some shoes? A blanket?" Was anyone listening? She'd been put into a plush room, but still. She hated being barefoot and wearing nothing but a thin silk robe.

"They're supposed to be coming for us." Analise sat on the pink bench. "This is comfy if you want to rest."

"No." She needed to keep moving. She'd incinerated Reuben and run away from Hermes. Her power truly was greater than she'd ever believed. But right now, she wanted closure and needed to be held.

"They could at least give us something else to wear." Analise rolled her eyes. "Think Pres is here?"

She hated hearing anyone else call him Pres, except Lance. "More than likely." He'd better be. If he was still frozen, she'd march right into Hermes' home and melt him in the same way she'd melted Reuben. No one would stand in her way.

A moment later, the door opened. A woman in a simple blue tunic and jeans stepped into the room. She smiled. "You must be Lulu and Analise."

"I am." She'd never seen such a beautiful woman. "This is… Analise."

Analise bowed. "My queen."

Queen? Shit. She'd already behaved wrong. "I should bow, shouldn't I?"

"No." The queen shook hands with both women. "You're fine. My name is Piper. I'm pleased to meet you. You've both been through quite an ordeal."

That was one way to put it. "We have." Lulu fidgeted with the knot on her robe. "We're safe now? That's what the big guy said."

"Diesel is his name, and you are. Ana, the elves will be pleased to know you're safe." Piper turned her attention to Lulu. "Your parents are happy you're safe, too."

"My parents?" They even knew she'd gone missing?

"The very ones. They, along with a certain satyr, are happy you're safe and sound," Piper said. "They knew quickly that you were gone."

A certain satyr. That warmed her heart. He'd known she was gone. "Is he here?"

"Preston?" Analise asked. "He's here?"

"He and Lance are, yes. Your parents -- for both of you -- are on the way." Piper snapped her fingers and the side door opened. "Be gentle. He's messed up and has been since you disappeared."

Lulu wished she could've had a shower and dressed in something less revealing. She braced herself for seeing Preston. Her heart beat for him and he owned part of her soul. All she'd wanted was to get back to him. Soon, she would.

Preston and Lance stepped into the room and Lance's eyes widened. Preston bowed his head.

"Lu." Lance embraced her. "I'm so glad to see you. We were so worried."

"I'm okay." She laughed as he squeezed her. He hugged so hard. She stared at Preston, who hadn't looked at her. What was wrong with him?

Lance let go, then hugged Analise. "Good to see

you. Are you okay?"

Analise nodded. "I'm fine. It's good to see you, too, Lance." She sighed. "Preston."

His shoulders sank as Preston looked up. The circles under his eyes seemed darker and the lines were etched onto his face. He kept space between him and Lulu. "Hi, girls."

"*Girls*?" Analise strode up to him. She rested her hands on her hips. "*Girls*? You haven't seen me in three years, and I'm just a *girl*?"

He flicked his gaze to Lulu, then closed his eyes.

Analise groaned. "You never were good at speaking up. You can flirt, but you can't commit."

Lance stepped between Analise and Preston. "Why don't you and I go over here? We need to talk, and they do, too."

"Do they?" Analise shook her head. "No. He was my boyfriend first. I get first dibs. We were going to get married. If he's going to choose either of us, he'd better be picking me."

Lulu rolled her eyes. She understood this scene all too well. There was no reason to get upset right now. He and Analise had to sort this out. She ventured over to Lance. "Hi."

"He's been through hell," Lance said. "Lost without you." He barely spoke above a whisper.

"I can tell." She turned her back on Preston. There was something different about him. Something she couldn't put her finger on.

"How are you, sweetheart? You look cold." Lance slipped his jacket off and offered it to Lulu. "At least warm up in this."

"Thanks." She threaded her arms into the jacket. The warmth from his body heat helped, but the garment smelled like him. She'd rather have something of Preston's. "She's been a mess without him, too."

"She picked Hermes." Lance shook his head. "This isn't fair."

"No, but they have to talk. I can't intervene or throw a fit. If he still has feelings for her, then he does." She wanted to cry. Losing him would be like losing her arm. Or her heart. "I'm afraid he still loves her." She couldn't handle it if he did.

"He did love her, but I don't know that he still does." Lance hugged her again. "Just don't let him get away. He's been a mess without you. He thought you were gone forever, and he'd never get you back. Thought he'd lost everything."

The information helped a little bit. She'd been destroyed without Preston, too. "Why couldn't he help me?"

"That's part of his curse. It's fucked-up, but our father punished both of us. He can't fall in love and if he does, he risks his girl. Only a woman who can see past his affliction will be the one for him. So far, no one has."

I have. She nodded. Didn't she count? "What if he finds someone who does?"

"Then his curse is lifted." Lance shrugged. "It's been a long time since he ever thought he'd find someone."

"I see." Not really.

Lance tipped his head and stared at her. "Do you love him?"

"I do." It wasn't a lie. "That's why I got away. I had to find him. His magic called to me. It's part of me." She sighed. She'd never be the same.

"His magic?" Lance snorted. "Then it all makes sense."

"What does?" she asked. Before she could say

more, a shriek caught her attention. She glanced over her shoulder.

Analise slapped Preston. "Never talk to me again. I hope you rot in Hades. Hell. I don't care. Just never... fuck you."

Lulu gasped but stayed rooted to the spot. She wasn't sure what to do. Lance surged forward and escorted Analise from the room. Within seconds, Lulu stood alone with Preston. He rubbed his face.

"Are you okay?" she asked. "She hit you pretty hard."

"It's just my face." He laughed, but she didn't detect any mirth in the sound. He shook his head. "She couldn't damage it too much."

"She could." If she didn't go to him, he'd never come to her. His pride had been stung too deeply. She crossed the room and slid her hand over his cheek. The skin was already red and shiny. He winced but didn't pull away.

"Pres." She threaded her free arm around him. "It's going to be okay. Whatever it is, it'll be okay."

"You don't know that. I hurt her." Preston finally met her gaze. "I told her the truth and she didn't want to hear it."

"The truth is hard to digest." She curled her fingers under his chin. She couldn't place the difference within him, but there was a change. "Pres?"

"I told her I'd been in love with her, but she'd walked away to be with him, so I moved on. She didn't like it. Said I'd forgotten about her. That's not true. I never forgot." He shook his head. "It's... a mess."

"You fell in love with someone else because she was gone. You assumed she'd never come back because she'd been incorporated into his world." She tipped his head to force him to look at her. "Now she's back and you're conflicted."

"I am."

She nodded. She wasn't about to give up without a fight, but she wasn't going to push him yet. "What does your heart want?"

"You."

The lack of hesitation pleased her. "Me?"

"You," he replied, his voice low. "Always have."

"At least since you met me." She brushed her thumb across his bottom lip. "I love you, Preston. With my whole heart, soul, and being. You're the one who brought out my magic, helped me tame it, and gave me a reason to get the hell out of that prison. Your curse, the one you had no control over, prevented you from helping me, but it gave me the incentive to get back here to break you out of it. I had to save you from yourself."

He wobbled and held onto her. "You have no idea."

"Don't I?" She wanted to understand.

"You broke the curse. I thought it was her, but it's always been you." He nodded to his legs. "No hooves."

She stepped back a bit to look at him and noticed the change. Feet, not hooves. Human legs, not hairy animal models. He wriggled his toes.

"See?" He held tight to her hand. "I thought it was because she'd come back. Thought maybe she'd been the one who caused it, but when I let my mind go, it went to you. You're my center and I told her that -- which upset her."

"I'm sure it did." But the knowledge pleased her. "Do you love me?"

"I do." He rested his forehead against hers. "You're my other half."

Then the trouble had been all worth it. "What do we do, then? You're mine and I'm yours." All she wanted to do was be with him. Shower, change and luxuriate in him. "Take me home?"

"To your apartment?"

"Ours." She couldn't imagine being anywhere else but with him.

"Your parents are arriving shortly." He squeezed her ass. "See them, then I'll take you home."

She didn't have much choice, but she'd make one demand. "Then I need to change. I'm not seeing my folks in this." She swept her hand over her attire. "I look terrible."

"I'm sure the queen can help with that." He embraced her and rested his forehead on hers. "I heard you scream. Felt you pull on me. My heart ripped in half."

"But you couldn't move."

"No," he whispered. "I felt helpless."

"You physically were, maybe, but your heart and power went with me." She slipped her hands into his back pockets. "I found something in me I didn't know I had. I managed to destroy Reuben. I ran from Hermes. The me who showed up in Eerie what seems like forever ago didn't have that strength. I do now. Because of you."

He grinned. "You're my strength, too." He nuzzled her nose and sighed. "Let's get you cleaned up. I need to meet the 'rents and you should have a proper outfit."

"As long as I'm with you, I'm just fine." Everything else would fall into place, just like it was supposed to be. She'd been taken by the satyr to every height she'd ever wanted. Not just taken -- but cherished. Loved.

Just as she should be.

* * *

Preston waited as Lulu disappeared with Piper. He hated being left alone, but he wanted her to be happy. Diesel joined him in the sitting room.

"Hi." Preston shifted in his seat. "She's getting dressed."

"I know. Pi loves to spoil people. She'll have Lulu polished to the nines." He shrugged. "But it'll be worth it. She deserves to be treated like a princess."

"She does." He'd make sure of it for as long as she'd have him.

"You're okay?"

He stared at Diesel. Was he okay? Sort of. He sighed and debated what to do. Confess or keep his mouth shut? "I'm nervous as hell." So much for quiet.

"About?"

"Her. Us. Meeting her family. What if they don't like me? I'm a fucking satyr." It sounded worse out loud.

"I'm a cyclops."

"You're the queen's consort." That made a big difference. He could get away with anything.

"I'm also looked at as a freak. Like you." Diesel glared at him. "She saw something in me I didn't. Lulu looks at you the same way. She sees something."

"She does." He wasn't sure what, but he thanked the gods she did. Still, he worried the curse hadn't truly been broken. He'd take off his socks and be a satyr again.

"Then trust that." Diesel swept his gaze over Preston. "It's already making a permanent difference."

It was? He frowned. "What?"

Diesel rolled his eye, then walked away.

Preston growled. What the hell... He strode over

to the couch and slumped onto the cushions. Why did Diesel have to tease him? They weren't exactly friends, but they weren't enemies. He flexed his toes and crossed his ankles. The nerve of the guy!

He looked down at his feet again. Yup. Sure enough, calf, ankle... foot... It wasn't a figment of his imagination. He hadn't dared to believe this was real until now. "Diesel!"

Instead of Diesel coming back into the room, Lulu ventured into the space. "What's wrong?"

"Still there. See?" He pointed to his feet. "You really did break the curse."

"I know." She smiled and grasped his hand. "I knew the moment we met you'd be fine. Knew it when we were reunited, but you had to believe it yourself."

"You did?" He'd barely thought they'd end up together, let alone the curse being broken.

"I did." She laughed. "Pres, my abilities told me you'd be fine, and you are."

The earnestness in her eyes warmed him to his core. He finally turned his attention to her outfit. Another sundress, clinging to her curves and a bit of makeup. "Beautiful," he murmured. "My Gods."

She squeezed his fingers. "I look okay?"

"Okay?" He wanted to take her to the closest bedroom and remove her dress to kiss every inch of her body. "Yes, you're more than okay. I want to make love to you right now."

"I like that, but you can't. We need to see Mom and Dad first." She beamed. "Because they're here." She turned as an elf and witch joined them in the room.

Shit. He tensed all over and wished he'd kept his boots and socks on. He had to look ridiculous. "You must be Lulu's parents. I'm Preston."

"The satyr." The elf extended his hand. "I'm

Daff, and this is my wife Dorinda."

He shook hands with the elf, then kissed the back of the witch's hand. "It's a pleasure to meet you."

"I hear you're quite fond of my daughter." Daff crooked his brow, but his smile lit up the room. "I'm glad. You're an interesting man."

Dorinda rolled her eyes after she hugged her daughter. "Satyr? A moment?"

Daff nudged Lulu and directed her away from Preston and Dorinda. Preston braced himself for whatever the witch had to tell him. He loved Lulu and he'd withstand whatever arrows Dorinda wanted to send, but he wasn't interested in fighting.

"Lulu is a powerful witch. I've never told her that, but she knows," Dorinda said. "I wanted to protect her, but I needed her to learn how to use that power to survive. If I'd have protected her, she wouldn't have escaped her demons."

"You're right." He nodded. "She wanted to be loved, though. Wanted to be with someone who cared about her, and she wasn't sure you cared. That's partly why she hooked up with Reuben and why my father butted in."

"I know. I could foresee it." Dorinda sighed and her auburn hair turned flame red. "I knew you'd walk into her life, too."

"You did?" Had she known Lulu would break the curse, too?

"All of it." She swept her gaze over him. "But I wasn't sure you'd make it work. Not just you. All of it. I worried Reuben would still destroy her, despite her abilities."

"She managed to win." He knew she would.

"She did," Dorinda said. "You're a good man. Sweet man. I've seen you at work. I've watched the way you are with her. You're kind to her. You care. I've never seen such devotion."

"Except with Daff." He'd seen that right away.

"Except him." Her smile shimmered a little bit. "You're a lot like Daff. Sweet, kind and willing to go to the floor for whomever you're with. I know you'll protect her."

"I will." Without a doubt.

"Then take care of her and help her become the best version of the witch she is." Dorinda stared at him, and her smile faded. "She needs a strong man behind her who can understand she needs his help but is willing to listen and let her fly. He gives her space to do what she needs. She loves you, but don't manipulate that love to make yourself look better."

"I won't." He had the strength and courage to be the man Lulu deserved because he knew himself. He'd been delivered from the curse, but he'd been given the love of a lifetime. He'd cherish her forever.

"Then you have my blessing for this union -- not that you needed it." She laughed, then shook her head and walked away. "Daff?"

"Yes, my love." Daff offered his arm, then nodded to both Lulu and Preston before leaving with Dorinda.

Lulu didn't move. "What just happened?"

"Your mother gave her blessing, but she also gave you the chance to be the most powerful witch you can ever be simply because she let you find that power yourself." He slid his hand along her back. "And you have. You're a great witch. You freed yourself and made friends with the queen. You did that. You freed me."

"I did." She embraced him. "But you were the spark. You showed me it's okay to be me. Okay to let my guard down."

"It is," he murmured. "And I'll never let you go. Never let you fall."

"I know you won't." She kissed him on the cheek. "Take me home, Pres. I want to go home."

"I'll take you wherever you want to go." Forever.

* * *

He should've made their excuses to the queen and Cyclops. Should've let them know he and Lulu were leaving, but he had the feeling they knew what was going on. He barely remembered the drive back to the apartment or even the race up to the front door. All he saw was Lulu.

The way the dress curved around her body, the way she smelled, the smile in her eyes and the sparkle emulating from her. He wanted to bottle this feeling. Never let it go.

He barely got to the bedroom with her before the need to make love to her overwhelmed him. He caged Lulu between his body and the bed, kissing along her throat, then down to her collarbone.

"Pres." She writhed beneath him. "More."

He'd give her plenty more. He arranged her legs around his waist, moving the dress high on her hips and exposing her. A gasp vibrated in his throat. "No panties?"

"Nope." She grinned and draped her arms around his shoulders. "They came off in the car."

"How…" He hadn't noticed. "I need you."

"You've got me." She snapped her fingers, undressing in seconds. She snapped her fingers again and undressed him, too. "Like that?"

"Convenient." He rubbed his hard cock against her pussy. The slickness was almost more than he could bear. How did she do this to him? Make him so crazy with desire and lust so fast?

"Make love to me, Pres." She arched again, trying to pull him into her body.

"Always." He pushed into her in one swift thrust, needing to make them one. The second he filled her he knew he'd found his home. He braced on his knees and hands, then worked into a steady rhythm. "Won't be slow."

"Don't want slow." She met him thrust for thrust.

He'd never be the same. She'd not only changed his body, but his heart. He believed in love, believed in forever and that his past wasn't the only thing to define him. His head swam, and the delicious pleasure of being with her overwhelmed him.

The sparkles filled the air and a soft yellow fog surrounded them. She cried out and dug her nails into his shoulders. "Pres."

"Here." He moved faster, losing himself in the pleasure of making love to her. When she looked into his eyes and whimpered, his heart beat just for her. She owned him. She'd freed him. Made him whole.

Lulu groaned and arched her back again. She closed her eyes. Red infused her cheeks as the lazy smile curled on her lips. A shiver rocked through her. She squeezed him tight within her body.

Every flutter and ripple of her pussy spurred him on. He fit within her so well, like she'd been made just for him. Maybe she had. Now he'd never have to let her go. Never have to lose her love. She belonged to him.

He cried out as the orgasm hit hard. The pleasure washed through him, forcing him to see how she'd given him wings. She'd made him fly. "Lu." He surged into her and embraced the orgasm. Nothing else mattered. The world melted, save for her.

She shivered again and relaxed her grip on his shoulders. She seemed to tremble in his arms. "Pres. Fuck."

"Let go, babe." He nuzzled her throat, then kissed a path along her jaw to her lips. He stared into her eyes. "My love."

She parted her lips and sighed. "You're mine, too. I love you, Preston."

"Love you, sweetheart." He slowed his thrusts, then stilled with her in his arms. He rested his forehead on hers. Her breath warmed his skin and tickled his cheeks.

She brushed her mouth over his. "You saved me."

"We saved each other." The sparkles evaporated, but the magic remained in the air. He pulled out and settled beside her on the bed. "Marry me."

She rolled onto her side, hooking her leg with his and draping her arm across his belly. "I've chosen you as my partner. My mate. My perfect match. We're sealed together."

"We are?" He liked that.

"Our magic chose each other. It's done and permanent." She sucked in a ragged breath. "I can't imagine being with anyone else."

"Neither can I. You're mine." He loved her with his entire being.

"My satyr," she murmured.

"Not a monster any longer." He stroked her cheek. "Just a man."

"You'll always be my satyr. The man who took me to the heights and helped me realize I've had love all along -- with him." She grinned. "Mine."

"I am yours." He hadn't expected life to turn out

this way. To find love with the most beautiful woman. Lulu truly was his other half and made him the best version of himself.

She'd proven love was possible and dreams could come true. He had his dream – his forever, with her.

Taken by the Valkyrie (Taken 6)
A Paranormal Women's Fiction Novella
Megan Slayer

Kara is tired of her role as a Valkyrie, not that she has much choice. Being a Valkyrie is her identity. It's in her blood. But she can only witness so much death and destruction. Her faith in humanity has waned.

Until she meets Eric.

Eric, a retired airman, is just as tired. He's seen things he believes no one else would understand. Then he picks up Kara, and his world is turned upside down. She's the one he never saw coming and the one he can't live without -- if only she can handle his past.

The past might be more than they can overcome, but what if these two warriors are exactly what they each need?

Chapter One

"Don't you dare get attached."

Kara folded her arms and groaned. She'd heard that line so many times through the centuries. What did attachments have to do with her? She wasn't about to hook up with anyone long-term again. She'd made that mistake once and nearly paid with her life. Not again.

Brynhildr glared at her. "You're not listening."

Kara snorted and shifted her attention from her thoughts to the elder Valkyrie. "You're right. I'm not." She mentally repeated the rules -- Valkyries are duty-bound, not permitted to form attachments, should stay free and vigilant.

Fine. Except she didn't want to be on duty any longer. The job had become too dangerous. She'd long tired of the blood, the gore, the anger. She'd retrieved so many warriors from the field of battle and delivered them to Valhalla, but she could only take the devastation for so long.

"I don't like you getting into scuffles in bars." Brynhildr shook her head and leaned her elbows on the high-top table. "You're looking for trouble. What do you have? A death wish?"

"What if I do?" She picked at the peanut shell remaining in the bowl. The bartender needed to replenish the snacks. When the monster came back around, she'd say something.

"What do you mean?" Brynhildr asked. "You're getting careless, like you're inviting trouble. You do know there's something big planned for you."

"Is there?" At least she didn't have to explain herself. She wasn't about to tell the elder she wanted to rest for a long time -- like forever. She'd contemplated final solutions a few times, but the idea of actually dying scared her. Her ex had tried to kill her, but she'd been reincarnated. Helgi swore he'd never let her forget him. She hadn't. But she also didn't want to be with him any longer.

"There's a plan for you, Kara. Don't jeopardize it." Brynhildr sighed and reached for Kara's arm. "What's got you so upset? Talk to me. You can't bottle it inside or you'll lose the battle."

She knew that all too well. Brynhildr was right. They did need to talk. "I don't want to retrieve any longer. I want a break. I can't handle the death and gore anymore. I'm tired of seeing so much pain. My heart can't take it. I don't want to settle down, but I need time away. I've thought about just ending it all to make the pain go away."

"Don't do that." Brynhildr squeezed Kara's bicep. "You're my dear friend. When you feel that way again, you tell me. I'll sit with you as long as you need and even when you don't."

"I know you will." She'd never doubted her friend and elder Valkyrie. "What's this big thing planned for me?"

"Promise me you'll call me when you get low." Brynhildr held tight to Kara's arm. "Promise."

"I will." She wouldn't go back on that.

"But you asked about the something big," Brynhildr said. "Not all warriors need to go to Valhalla. Some need care here first. It's up to you if you're interested in giving that care before they can go. It doesn't mean they're on the battlefield. In some cases, they're still fighting even though they're home."

"Still?" she murmured. Someone else understood what she saw when she closed her eyes?

"You might even find yourself along the way."

She hadn't expected the elder to say that. She'd expected to stay lost and drift away. But if she could help someone, that would be good -- if she could even help. Most people were afraid of her. What if the person she was supposed to assist didn't want her help? What if they didn't like her?

"We have someone specific in mind for your first job. What if I could tell you what he looks like?" Brynhildr asked. "Could show you?"

"You could?" Now the elder had her full attention. "Show me."

"Are you interested in taking a different route and helping him?"

She hesitated. She should say no and return to sulking. "I am." The words spilled off her tongue. She didn't hear the undercurrent of conversation in the bar, didn't smell the cigarettes and stale beer in the air, or even notice the smoke swirling around her. Her senses hyper-focused on what Brynhildr said. "I want to see him."

"Very well." Brynhildr produced a mirror.

The image of a man formed in the glass. Brown hair, crinkles around his brown eyes, tension in his posture, too thin, but handsome. Kara narrowed her eyes. He was damn cute, but wasn't he off-limits? "I can't get attached to him?"

"You know the code."

She did. She also wasn't entirely sure what he'd be like. He might be a jerk. Have the personality of a brick. Or he could be damn sexy, enticing, and sweet. Just lost too. He could be the kind of man a woman wanted to chase, to wrap up in, and never let go. The kind she wanted to kiss, touch, and tease. To feel moving inside her.

Not the perfect man -- but damn close.

If he really existed.

He might not.

There wasn't much point in getting her hopes up.

"Just don't fall in love." Brynhildr shook her head. "Remember how that worked out with Helgi? This one might be a better fit and not nearly so violent, but you're a proud Valkyrie, and you should remain unattached."

"I should." She'd followed the rules during this life. Previous ones? Not so much. This time around, she wanted to be a good Valkyrie. A proud one. She didn't have time for romance. No time to waste on something that wasn't going to last.

What if it did? What if this wasn't just a passing fancy? What if they fell in love?

She had to stop thinking like this. Just because falling in love was possible didn't mean it'd happen. Falling on her head was just as possible. Gods, it was more believable. She wasn't a kid and didn't need love. Right?

Everyone could live without love and affection.

What if she didn't want to any longer? What if she wanted to be romanced? What if he had the key to her happiness, and he held the key to her heart? Only the power of the gods could show her that truth. Where was a god when she needed one?

"He's here in Eerie. I'll bet you've seen him," Brynhildr said. "Don't spook him. I know you're good at being blunt."

"I'll be tender." She left her chair before the elder could give her extra instructions. She needed to run. To get the fuck out of the bar and stretch. Besides, the call of duty was too strong.

She shouldn't head to the fields, but the innate desire pulled too hard. The moment she broke into a run, her stomach roiled. Going to the fields wasn't just a desire. It was part of her. Part of being a Valkyrie. She was there to fight. To protect. To bring the warriors to Valhalla.

Her muscles ached, and tension pulled tight in her shoulders. As much as she needed to be there, she hated it. She'd rather visit the warrior who needed her off the battlefield, but first, she had to go to the front.

When she arrived, the smell of smoke filled the air. The bombs were larger and the means of war more destructive, but the anger never changed. It was always at the highest level. She moved around the vehicles. An acrid smell filled her senses. She shuddered. She knew that tang -- death.

Time to work.

She rushed to the serviceman's side. What he did, where he associated -- that didn't matter. This was war, and he'd been hit in battle. The other warriors tried to offer comfort to the soldier, but she knew the truth. He wasn't going to make it.

She winced when she saw the wound. He'd been hit by a fragment, his femoral artery slashed. He'd bleed out before the tourniquet would work. His screams filled her ears, and the booms from the other artillery fire drowned out the rest of the world.

She leaned over the warrior and touched his chest. No one else could see her -- not when she did this job. She smiled, offering comfort, but knowing nothing could help much now. She held her hand over his heart. The gesture was one of her own, not from the code of Valkyrie. She wasn't even sure if there was a code, but she'd been at this for so long she'd forgotten the rules. The one thing she never ignored, though, was kindness.

"You're going home." She splayed her fingers

over his chest. "It's time to come with me now." No one else could see or hear her. Just him and only in this moment. Once he made it to Valhalla, she'd disappear because he was home.

"You're real?" A sad smile curled on his lips, and a tear slipped down his dirty cheek. "I'm tired."

"I know. It's okay to let go." She held his hand. As she stepped back, she tugged lightly on him. His body remained, but his soul followed her. She spread her wings and held tightly to him.

"I haven't told them goodbye," he said and wrapped his arms around her. "Do they know?"

"They do." She flew them to Valhalla and within seconds, landed among the other warriors. "You're home."

He stared at her a moment. His body, once broken and mangled from the bombing, was now whole. He wore his dress uniform with the medals and ribbons on his chest. As if he finally realized what was going on, he stood taller and saluted her. "Thank you."

"You're welcome." She nodded once, then disappeared. He'd never remember her, not that she minded. The job wasn't meant to be memorable -- not for her. She headed back to the battle, but for the time being her services weren't needed. Good.

She headed home, but the weight of sadness, destruction, and death wore on her. The tension filled her mind. She hadn't paid much attention to the battlefield. Never did. Seeing the devastation was too much. At one time, she'd taken the care to notice every detail. But seeing the same general scene, something blown to bits, something destroyed, something on fire. The screams, the chaos, the body parts where they weren't supposed to be. She couldn't stomach it any longer.

She landed on her feet in Eerie and bowed her head. When she delivered a warrior home, she always stopped a moment to give thanks for his or her service. She also paused to beg the world to forget about war. No more fighting. Put her out of a job. For good.

When she looked up, she noticed the vehicle, an olive-green Jeep. Most of the cars and trucks in Eerie weren't so normal. Why have something like everyone else when one could use magic to add flair?

She watched the driver, the man from the image. She wasn't sure how old he was, but he seemed to have all his hair and a bit of scruff. The air of sadness radiated to her. She wanted to talk to him. He was the one she'd been sent to save.

He stopped the Jeep and exited the vehicle. The way he carried himself, his stride and confidence, spoke volumes about his character. Seeing him at his full height, she knew this was the guy.

He seemed to look in her direction but didn't appear to see her. No matter. She wasn't ready to be seen yet. She needed to study him. Figure him out. Help him. Find a way for him to heal. She nearly raced across the street to him. Nearly. If she rushed up to him right now, she'd spook him.

The man tensed and yanked his phone from his front pocket. She couldn't hear what he said.

She longed to touch him. To slide her arm around him and feel the softness of his skin, the scrape of his beard on her cheek, and see the color of his eyes. To look into those eyes and feel needed.

He might not want her. He could be married or not interested.

That didn't matter. She wasn't ready for love or commitment. She'd rather get to know him and see if the crackle she felt was real.

For now, she'd simply watch. There would be time later to talk to him. When it came, she'd be ready. No matter what, she'd be ready.

Chapter Two

Eerie had never felt like home, but then again, nowhere else did either. Eric shook his head. He'd spent years going from place to place, settling anywhere from a few months to a few years. The military bases were fine but tended to be cold, utilitarian places. He didn't have a family, so he didn't always fit in anywhere.

He still didn't have anyone and wasn't sure he wanted to put down roots, but he'd often been drawn to Eerie. The place had a power to it. Like he was supposed to be there. Why? He wasn't entirely sure. He knew the stories. The town existed for supernatural and paranormal creatures.

Eric Whitrock sure as fuck wasn't paranormal.

A simple airman who liked to work with aircraft and mind his own business. He loved people-watching, too. A person could learn a lot by watching his or her surroundings. What people did, where they went, who they went with and how. The tendency to pay attention kept him safe in most situations. But not all.

He winced. He'd been through a lot in his forty-five years. Too much. He'd seen friends move away, transferred, quit… or what had happened to them that terrible day.

He'd never get that afternoon out of his mind.

When he thought about the past, the darkness enveloped his thoughts. The depression tended to drag him down.

Not today. He refused to give in. He'd wasted a lot of time on things he couldn't change.

So why come to Eerie? There wasn't anything there for him.

Too bad his heart didn't agree. Neither did whatever force within him that kept dragging him back to town. He didn't understand the pull and wasn't about to question it. If he'd learned anything in life, it was that sometimes things weren't meant to be solved and others weren't meant to be understood.

Just go with the flow.

That flow brought him back to Eerie. He drove along the main thoroughfare to the edge of the business district. The bars along the road illuminated the right of way better than the streetlights.

A figure came into view. Seeing her drew a deep need within him to protect her. He had no idea who she was, but he couldn't let her walk.

He slowed and rolled down the window. "Do you need help?"

She stopped walking. When she turned to look at him, he noted her torn shirt, the dirt on her jeans and missing shoes. The wildness in her eyes bothered him, but not as much as the smear of blood -- which he hoped wasn't hers -- on her cheek.

"Let me help you," he said and opened the Jeep door. "Please? Who are you trying to get away from?"

She didn't speak and instead jumped into the vehicle. She slammed the door behind her. The shivering and the way she tucked herself down in the seat bothered him.

"Where to?" He drove away from the location, not sure where to go.

"I don't care." She stared at him. "Just go."

"You've got it." He sped down the road toward the outskirts. "Are you okay?"

"No." She continued to shiver. The bell on the dash dinged to signal her lack of safety restraints. "What'd I do wrong?" she asked.

"You should buckle up." He kept going but turned onto the side road and rushed toward the residential area. The shifter village tended to be safer -- so he'd been told. Then again, who would want to tangle with a pissed-off wolf shifter? Not him.

He slowed to a respectable speed. "Are you okay? Do I need to get you aid?" He should take her to the hospital. "You're bleeding."

"It's not mine." She sat up a bit and sighed. "Not all of it."

"What happened?" He kept glancing over at her while he drove. "How did you get hurt?"

"Would you believe it's nothing?"

"No." Not a chance.

"I didn't think so." She plugged the belt end into the buckle. "I don't want to drag you into this."

"Consider me dragged." He wasn't a man of honor. Not at all. He'd spent too many days baking in the sun and too many nights trying to forget his problems. "I won't let whoever hurt you do it again."

"You won't?" Her eyes widened. "You don't know me."

"Don't have to know you to know you're in danger. I won't let anyone hurt you." It was a gut-deep response, one he wasn't sure how to stop.

She balled her hands. "I'm trying to run away."

"From?" He shouldn't push, but he wasn't about to let her go back to something dangerous.

"Look, you don't want to know or get involved with me. I'm not the kind of girl a guy wants around." She shook her head again. "More like the one you want to stay far, far away from."

"I disagree." He barely knew her but already worried about her. "You're bleeding."

She sighed. "I've got a man chasing me, but it's

fine. He tries to catch me, and I won't let him. I won't ever let that bastard hurt me. He tries, but he fails because I can take care of myself."

"If you don't want him bothering you, then don't let him." He kept driving. "But I can't just let you go. You're hurt."

"You have no idea." She pointed. "I need to go there."

"The castle?" He could've sworn she pointed to the hotel-slash-castle. "I can take you there."

"No." She pointed again, this time to a darkened house. "There."

Before he could truly slow down, she threw the door open and jumped out of the Jeep.

"Wait." He screeched to a halt. "Please?"

She rushed up to the front door and disappeared into the house. He blinked, barely registering she'd been there. Like a ghost.

Did ghosts exist in Eerie? She'd come into his life and was gone so quickly.

The aura of something remained in the Jeep. Flowery. Her perfume? Seemed like. He hadn't had any other women in the vehicle lately. He stopped at the first traffic light and glanced over at her seat. A drop of blood remained against the back.

His worry increased. What had her so upset? An ex? Something worse? He wasn't sure. He hadn't even gotten her name. So much for his keen observational skills.

He made his way around the neighborhood once more, checking on the house she'd gone into before driving away. The lights were out and the place appeared abandoned. He debated marching up to the front door, but what good would that do? Probably freak her out even more. If the place was dark, it could be to hide from whomever was chasing her. Fool them into believing she wasn't there.

Against his better judgment, he drove to the castle in town. Despite visiting Eerie more than a dozen times, he'd never bothered to get an apartment. He didn't live there. Just visited.

Where could someone go when they wanted to visit? The hotel.

Eerie just happened to have an old castle as the best lodgings. He parked in the courtyard lot, then made his way to the front desk. No bags, just himself. So sad.

He walked up to the counter. He'd been there half a dozen times, but never tired of the whimsy. The counter sparkled, the scent of flowers lingered in the air, and the soft pink lighting added to the ambiance. The place was massive, too. He wondered how the management was able to keep the large building clean.

The faerie behind the desk smiled. She wasn't the same woman who'd been there before. "Welcome to Eerie. How long will you be staying?"

He hadn't thought about that. "I don't know."

"You don't?" She tapped the counter. "Well, I have two long-term suites, if you're interested."

"Long-term?" He dug in his front pocket for his wallet. "I'm interested."

"Good." She grinned, and he swore electricity zapped around her. He wasn't drawn to her. But he hadn't been drawn to many people for a long time. He'd shielded himself from the world, trying to stay safe. Getting too close to anyone meant letting them in and allowing them to see his disaster. No one needed to see that.

"Here's your key. We like to stay a bit old-school in that respect, but I'll get you your passcode as well."

She slipped him a piece of paper. "I've already registered you and added your information to the database."

He fumbled and shoved his wallet back into his pocket. "You've got my info on file?"

"In a way." She swept her hand in front of him. "My power is information retention and gathering. I don't need to see your cards to know who you are or to charge you."

"Dangerous." He wasn't a fan of her power. "Scary."

"Which is why I work here and not anywhere else." She shrugged. "I'm bound to the hotel now. No one wants a faerie around who can glean information. What if I get someone's credit card number? Learn their spells? I might not be trustworthy. I am, but few beings believe that."

"I understand." Not really, but he wasn't about to argue.

She flattened her hands on the counter. "So, I've got you set up for a suite on the fourth floor. Bedroom, living space, kitchenette, and big bathroom."

"I need the code, right?" He wasn't sure he could afford a suite, but oh well. It was just money… it grew on trees.

"Here." She offered him a card. "The code is embedded in that with a spell. If you need anything, just let me know. I'll be sure to handle the problem. By the way, what you're worried about will sort itself out. The money, the other situation… it'll be fine. You'll find what you're looking for here."

"Peace of mind?" he blurted. "Sorry."

"Maybe." She grinned. "I can't see the future, but I can tell you're on a journey, and not because you're at a hotel. Because you're searching for something. I can't see what you're going to find, but I can tell you it'll be worth the trouble. Don't give up."

"Thanks." He didn't want a motivational poster-style speech, but he'd been given one. He accepted the card and wandered away from the desk, then thought, *I didn't ask for the room number.*

"Room Four-Oh-Eight," the faerie called. "I got you."

He waved to thank her, then went to the elevator. As he pressed the button, awaiting the car, he let his thoughts wander, but not for long. He checked over his shoulder. The way she'd read his mind bothered him. It knocked him off his guard and he hated that. He prided himself on paying attention.

The car opened, and he checked over his shoulder. No one seemed to be following him, but he'd never gotten rid of the feeling he was being watched. Maybe it was the guilt following him around. The need for vigilance. He wasn't sure.

He stepped into the elevator and pounded the button to close the doors. There wasn't another soul around, but he refused to share the car. The sudden ascension made his stomach lurch. When the doors opened again, he stood on the fourth floor. At least he was almost to his temporary home.

He rushed down the corridor to the correct room, the suite, then swiped his card. After a couple of quick glances up and down the hallway, he darted into the room. The moment he stepped in the room, his heart raced. To be honest, his heart rate had been out of control all along.

He grabbed the remote and turned on the television. The show didn't matter. Only the noise did. He pushed the chair from the dinette in front of the door, wedging the back of the seat against the handle.

He engaged the lock and chain, then placed his hand on the metal surface. For one of the few times in his life, he wished he knew magic to put a charm on the door.

He kicked out of his shoes and sat on the bed. Sleep filled his brain, but he doubted he'd give in. He rarely succumbed. He needed the rest, yet he couldn't shut off his thoughts. When he closed his eyes, he was transported back to the day of the disaster. The vigilance hit hard. He could still hear the thunder of bombs and smell the acrid smoke. He shivered. No matter how hard he tried, he'd never forget.

He collapsed against the mattress and stared at the ceiling. Another thought popped into his mind. The girl from the drive.

He couldn't settle knowing she was out there and unsafe. Who the fuck wanted to hurt her? Why wasn't she safe? He needed to know. The edginess increased the more he worried. He wanted to find her. Bring her home. Give her peace of mind.

He'd thought he'd come to Eerie to rest, but maybe not. He wouldn't be settled until he'd found her and ensured she'd be okay. Tall order? Maybe impossible.

Chapter Three

Kara woke the next morning and stretched. For the first time in as long as she could remember, she'd slept. What a strange concept. Sleep. Not just sleep, but actual rest. She left her bed and showered, then dressed.

"Going out?" Brynhildr asked. "I know you saw him."

"I did. He's nice."

"*Nice*?" Brynhildr crooked her brow. "I don't get the feeling you just met him. You scared the shit out of him. I saw how you returned to the house last night. Did you run into Helgi?"

She stopped short, and tension settled between her shoulders. "Yes."

Helgi had been there. He'd found her. She didn't want to think about talking to him. He wasn't supposed to have been at the battle. Wasn't supposed to be fighting or recognize her.

But he had.

He'd seen her, chased her, and damn near torn her apart. The passion wasn't in his eyes. No, this was raw anger.

"What did he say to you?" Brynhildr put her cup down. "Did he threaten you?"

"Maybe." She tried to be nonchalant, but it wasn't easy. "I'm fine."

"He threatened you. He was supposed to be your true love."

"He's not the same man he was." She wrapped her arms around her body. "Time, as well as his life experiences, haven't been kind to him."

"I know they haven't." The elder Valkyrie crossed the room and stood beside her, but not touching. "You've changed, too."

"I have." She wasn't the wide-eyed girl she'd been when she and Helgi had first met. Love was real, but it wasn't supposed to hurt. As the years rolled by, he'd become someone else, and his temper flared. He still knew her but spent less time trying to find her. When he succeeded, he pursued her relentlessly. She could wait until he landed in battle, and the cycle continued toward his demise. But what good would that do? He'd come back. She wasn't sure how. He'd chased her so many times.

"Has he hurt you?" Brynhildr whispered.

"He tried." She refused to say his name. The less she said about him, the better the chances he'd disappear for good.

"And?"

"I stopped him." She cleared her throat. "But I ran into the soldier." She had to change the subject.

"I know you did." Brynhildr sighed and folded her arms. "And? Is he cute?"

"He is." She matched the elder's stance. "He's sweet, too."

"Oh?"

She should come clean about the meeting. If anyone would understand, it was Brynhildr. The elder had loved and lost, and never seemed to have gotten over it. A fresh start would do them all good. "I had been doing my job. I delivered four last night, but after the last one, Helgi spotted me."

Kara bowed her head. "He tried to grab me, and I had to tuck and roll down a hill to get away. I ended up filthy, my shirt torn, and my jeans stained. Sucked. I ran until my chest ached. When I came out onto the main road, I saw the Jeep. The soldier. He stopped to help me and didn't question me when I jumped into the vehicle. Not even a hesitation. He brought me home."

"That was dangerous."

She shrugged. When she'd felt him near, she knew she'd be okay. He wasn't a threat. "My soul knew him." That wasn't the right thing to say, but she'd done it.

"Soul?" Brynhildr crooked her brow. "Not you, too? You're not falling for that soulmate business! It's not the truth. It's a fib we tell our children to make them kinder to each other, but it means little. Helgi was never your soulmate, and you can't know that about the soldier."

"You're right," Kara replied. "He's not. I don't know if the soldier is, either. He could be a wrong turn, but I can't deny the pull. He would've come home with me if I'd asked. He would be here right now protecting me. Not because of some duty. It was the magic." She wasn't sure how to explain this. She'd been drawn to him.

"Magic?"

"He's para -- I don't know what -- but I felt it."

Brynhildr just stared at her.

"I felt safe when I was with him. I can't explain why." She'd also felt sad, confused, and so connected to him. Like they'd been through something together.

"Just keep your head on your shoulders. You're here to help him. To get him to his version of Valhalla. Don't mess that up. It's an honor to guide the warriors."

"I know." She took her job seriously, and despite the fact he wasn't dying -- at least she didn't think he was -- she still needed to be near him. "I'm going to find him."

"I have no doubt," Brynhildr said. "Just don't

spook him. I can't tell why, but he's a special case. He needs to be handled with care."

"I will." She left the counter and crossed the house to the front table where she picked up her purse, phone, and keys. A walk would do her good. So would a cup of coffee. "Don't wait up."

"It's only half past nine in the morning," Brynhildr called. "Be safe."

She would. Kara left the house after donning her shoes. Some days, she loved the late spring air. The crispness and the scent of flowers around her gave her comfort. She liked being able to stretch and be free. Mornings like this reminded her there was good in the world. Not everything amounted to death and destruction.

Still, she kept an eye out. Helgi had found her once and he could locate her again.

She'd rather run into the soldier. At least he gave off an air of safety.

Kara picked up her pace and strode to the coffee shop. If anything, she wanted the caffeine to keep her awake while she searched. Where would the soldier hang out? Did he even live in Eerie? So many questions and so few answers. She needed to know his name.

She yanked the door open to the shop, then headed inside. When she glanced around at the various patrons, she saw him. Talk about luck. The soldier sat alone in the corner with his back against the wall. She sensed the warrior within him. She also felt the aura of sadness, confusion, and hurt around him. Would he speak to her?

Someone dropped a cup and the clatter of porcelain on the tile floor split the air. Conversation stopped for a moment. She tensed but noticed the soldier's actions. Not only did he tense up, he also shot away from the table and hustled out of the shop.

Kara abandoned the line and followed him to the sidewalk. Good thing she'd kept in shape, otherwise matching his pace would've been impossible. He walked so fast. As she followed him, she paid attention to his moves. He seemed to be looking all around, hands jammed in his jacket pockets and strides long. He ducked behind a tree near the rock wall.

She wondered what he seemed to be running from. She wanted to approach him, but she opted for caution. He'd been through something and was on a hair-trigger.

Despite her better judgment to leave him alone, she rounded the wall. He sat with his back against the rocks. She held up both hands. "Hi. I saw you leave and hoped you were okay."

"Yeah." His brow furrowed, but he didn't remove his sunglasses. "I'm fine."

"I can tell you are now. May I sit with you?" she asked and put her hands down.

He seemed to stare at her. "Sure."

She moved slowly and sat beside him. For the first time since she'd run into him, she got a good look at him. Dark hair, aviator glasses, not that she was surprised -- many warriors sported those glasses -- muscles, his hands balled tight. She noticed his hands. He didn't have tough workman hands, but rather nice ones. She'd always been a sucker for nice hands. He wore work boots and jeans but hid his upper body with a leather jacket.

Was he a pilot? She wasn't in the mood to deal with another moody pilot. They were damn good at their jobs but could be such prima donnas.

She liked the timbre of his voice, though. Commanding and in control, but soft. "I'm not wild

about loud noises. They freak me out and remind me…
They remind me of stuff. I served with the V unit." It
wasn't a total lie, but she doubted anyone had a V unit.
The Valkyries did.

"You served?" He didn't look at her. Instead, he
seemed to stare off into space.

"I did. You?" she asked. Was he trying to keep an
eye on his surroundings? She'd bet so. "I did.
Fulfilling, but hard stuff." Again, not a lie. She'd seen a
lot of shit in her life. "You?"

"Nineteen years."

"That's a long time." She faced him. She'd served
much longer, but she was a lot older. As she swept her
gaze over him, she wondered what para blood he had
running through his veins. She didn't detect elf,
gnome, or witch. Didn't see any signs of faerie, either.
"Where did you serve?"

"Jordan and Qatar. Refueling." His voice came
out flat. "Was fine."

She'd learned over the years how the warriors
would talk about some things, but not all and when
they did initially talk, it wasn't with much inflection.
"Yeah?" He didn't sound fine, though. He sounded
sad. She wanted to get him to open up -- in his own
time. "How long have you been out?"

"Six years."

Another flat response. "Nice."

"You? Are you out?"

She hadn't expected him to ask that. Most
warriors didn't give a shit about her life. But
considering the time she came to them, there wasn't
much space to chat. "I've been out for ten years." It
wasn't the entire truth. She'd served for centuries, but
he wasn't going to understand that right now.

He turned his head and seemed to look at her,

but she wasn't sure. "Oh? How long did you serve?"

"Fifteen years." Another lie, but it wasn't the time to be truthful. Once she knew he understood what she was, then she'd tell him everything. If he didn't understand anything about paranormals, then nothing she'd tell him about the truth would make sense.

"You don't look old enough to have that much time under your belt," he said. "You barely look out of your twenties."

She'd been told that. She had control over her looks. If she wanted to appear older, then she could, but why? "How old do you think I am?" Besides ancient. Whatever he said, she'd agree.

"Forty?"

Close enough. "I'm forty-four." Hopefully he wouldn't do the math. "You?"

"Forty-seven."

He'd given her information she'd bet he normally kept tight to his chest. She held out her hand. "My name is Kara." She figured he'd remember her from the night before. How could he not? Part of her wanted him to forget her, but the rest of her was happy he hadn't.

"Are you okay?" he asked. "You seem in better spirits and don't appear to have any wounds."

"It was mostly dirt." She flattened her hands on her lap. "I'm sorry I worried you."

"You did. I thought you were in danger."

"I was." She couldn't look away. No one else had ever been concerned about her. Helgi hadn't been. He'd wanted to control her.

"Then why didn't you let me take you somewhere safe?"

His voice had an edge to it she didn't like, but she wasn't about to show emotion yet. "I was safe at the house. I'm not safe at night when I'm out, but getting home helped. You did that." She tipped her head. "Will you at least tell me your name? I'd like to properly thank my rescuer."

"Eric," he said softly. He stuck his hand out to her. "Kara, it's nice to meet you."

"It's good to know you, too." She swore sparks shot through her system. She opened her mouth to speak, but no sound came out. The electricity was almost too much for her to handle. She'd never felt such a pull like this. After a moment, she caught hold of her composure. "Thank you for taking me home. I'm sorry I scared you like that, but I'm glad you came along."

"I am, too," he replied. "Who or what were you running from? You don't look beat up. It was really just dirt?"

She shrugged. If he wanted to hide his past, then she wasn't about to share all of hers, either. "It was dirt." Like she'd tell him she healed in an instant. He'd never believe her. "I was running from my past." Shit. She hadn't planned to say that, but the words tumbled out. Normally, she kept this kind of information to herself. Looking at him and her reflection in his glasses must've been some sort of truth serum.

"Does it follow you often?" he asked.

"Yes." Everywhere. "Like a shadow." It wasn't a lie. The pain from her job, the terrible things she'd witnessed and the incidents with Helgi were never far from her mind.

"Mine, too."

"Yeah?" She'd let him open up when ready, but she'd be there when he did. "Mine never lets up."

"Do you need a safer place to stay? From him or her?"

She already lived with the other Valkyries, but she didn't want to stay with them for much longer. Not when a better offer presented itself. Besides, Helgi hadn't found her again -- not yet. He would. "I could. Do you know a safer house?"

"Safer than the one I took you to?" he asked. "I do."

She let go of his hand, finally realizing she'd been holding it this long. Then again, he hadn't released her hand, either. "Oh? Where?"

"Mine."

She bit back a gasp. "Should I trust you?" He wasn't Helgi. He was the warrior, Eric. He needed her. But should she go home with him already? She had her doubts.

"Soldiers never let each other down, never leave anyone behind. I'm an airman, not a marine, but it's true. I won't leave you behind, and I won't let you be hurt."

A gentleman. She wasn't used to those. She hadn't come in contact with one who wasn't dying in a long time. "You don't have to. You don't owe me anything and don't have to save me." But he was a warrior. So was she. She was supposed to save herself and others. She should be working -- not flaking off because she wanted a break. Valkyries didn't need breaks. Right?

"Just because I don't have to doesn't mean I won't. I saw the blood and you looked miserable. Like a scared doe. Are you okay?" He held out his hand again. "I've got you."

She had no doubt he did. She should say no, but she did a lot of things she shouldn't and didn't do many she should. "I'm not okay, but I'm surviving."

"That doesn't answer my question."

She knew it didn't. "You're right. You're also right that I'm in danger. I'm tired of running and tired of hiding. I can take care of myself, but if you're not going to budge and want me to trust you, then I will." She accepted his hand again and the sparks came right back. They were stronger than before, actually. She sucked in a ragged breath. Touching him had a rush like being in battle -- fighting for her side and taking a warrior to Valhalla. A rush like she'd never felt. Not even with Helgi. He didn't say anything and instead caressed the top of her hand with the pad of his thumb.

"Hi." She wasn't sure why she'd said that. She'd already met him, but it was like they'd never met before.

"Hi." His eyes widened, then softened and he smiled. "You're an old soul."

What an odd thing to say, but he was right. "I told you I was forty-four."

"You did, but there's something in your eyes. You look so young, but in that time, you've seen a lot. It's a heavy burden." His smile softened. "You don't have to carry it alone."

She'd wanted to hear that for so long. "Most of us have."She squeezed his fingers. "Would you take me home? I could use a warrior to protect me. I'd love to have someone to talk to. I've got a lot to say."

"I'm sure you do," he replied. "You have my word."

"Thank you." She'd stepped into something deeper than she'd ever expected, but she wasn't afraid. For the first time in a long while, she looked toward the future. She wasn't alone. "Are you ready for this story?"

He nodded. "I am."

Then so was she.

Chapter Four

Eric stared at Kara. He'd allowed her to touch him. Not only touch him, but hold onto him. He shivered, despite not being cold. He couldn't remember the last time he'd been this close to anyone.

She understood him better than most people. She had to be some sort of angel. "Are you an angel?" he blurted. The words weren't supposed to come out, but they had.

"No." She chuckled. "Far from it."

He nodded, debating what to say next. He wanted to hear her story, but he also needed to do some talking. Her touch wasn't odd or foreign. Wasn't scary, either. Hell, she aroused him. Something he'd thought was long dead. She comforted him with her caress.

"I'm sorry," he replied. "I don't know why I said that."

"It's okay." She caressed his hand again. "Why'd you leave the service?"

"It was the right time. You?" He hadn't opened up much about that time in his life, but she made it easy.

"The right time. I needed a break."

A car backfired and the sound split the air. He ducked, despite sitting behind the wall. *Call it conditioning.* He winced, wishing she couldn't see him or feel his tension.

"You okay?"

"The noise." Another thing he wasn't ready to talk about, but he'd explained it to her -- even if only in a small part.

"It's deafening sometimes." She stared at him. "When I was in, I helped with recovery. The things you see. It's rough. I loved my job, but after a while, it got to be hard. I wasn't ready to see one more mutilated body. What people do to each other…"

He didn't push her to keep talking, but he didn't tell her to stop. If she wanted and needed to talk, then he'd listen. He continued to hold her hand, but not just for her comfort. For his own reassurance.

"It's funny. Not ha-ha funny, but sad funny. I got used to the distraction. Got used to the horror," she murmured. "Got used to death."

"Kara." He wanted to take the pain and sadness from her. He knew how it felt to live with it. Some days the heaviness threatened to take him under.

"Too much?"

He shook his head. "I get it." But he wasn't ready to talk just yet. "You were with recovery?"

"I was. When someone fell, it was my job to help retrieve them."

"A medic?" He'd been friends with a few of them and loved that they did their job. He wasn't medic material.

"Not exactly."

His job wasn't easy, but hers had to have been almost impossible.

"I told myself to think of it as my duty. Don't give up. Do your duty because they depend on you."

"They do."

She sighed and rubbed her knee. "Do you know what I did? I took soldiers to Valhalla. Every beaten, battered, destroyed-in-battle warrior. I helped them." She balled her hand. "I'll bet you don't believe it."

He hesitated a moment to really take in what she'd said. Valhalla. Her name was Kara. She'd taken soldiers to Valhalla… Was she a Valkyrie? He suppressed a snort. Well, no kidding, she'd be a

Valkyrie. This was Eerie. Anything was possible. And he was there, too. She deserved to know what he was -- if only he knew himself.

"You're not surprised? Not disgusted?" she asked. "Talk to me."

"There's nothing to be surprised about," he replied. "I don't know what to say, but it's not a total shock. This is Eerie, and anything is possible here. My neighbor at the hotel is a gnome, and the woman behind the counter is a faerie. I have a friend who's a witch and another who's half elf. It's not beyond reason that you're a Valkyrie." He couldn't believe he'd said all that, but she needed reassurance. He could do that.

"You're really not shocked?"

"Nope." He'd heard some really out-there things, but this wasn't one of them. "Should I be?"

Her brows knitted and she frowned. "You should, because everyone else is shocked. They fear me. When they see me coming, they think it must mean someone's dying."

That made sense. "Am I?"

"No." She offered him a soft smile. "You're not."

"Are you off duty?"

"Something like that."

He nodded again. "You've seen some really messed-up stuff." And it made so much more sense why she'd be so tired. His nightmare had taken place over one afternoon. Hers was never-ending. "Is that what you ran from?"

"No." She let go of him and wrapped her arms around her body. "That's a whole different story."

"I'm listening if you want to tell me." He shouldn't push her. "I've seen things -- not on your scale, but I have. Most of the time, I just want to forget."

"I'm sure you do."

He'd hidden for so long. "I need to deal with my past." He summoned personal strength he hadn't been sure he still possessed. "You need shelter."

"I do."

"I offer shelter." Despite his better judgment, he stood and held out his hand. "Come with me."

"You still want me?" She slipped her hand into his and allowed him to tug her to her feet. "I'd like to go with you, if the offer is still good."

"It is." He fell into step with her and twined his fingers with hers. "May I cook for you?" He hated to admit his love language was food, because many people hadn't liked that show of emotion. Kasey hadn't.

"Cook?" She bumped shoulders with him and kept walking. "Are you any good?"

"I do my best." He could read a recipe and follow directions. Sometimes he even experimented a bit.

"I'd love that."

He couldn't hold back the snort. She'd surprised him as much as she'd thought she'd shocked him. "Then I would love to cook for you. You'll come with me?"

"I'd follow you anywhere."

She could be suggesting something bigger than he could handle, but he wasn't afraid. For once, he wasn't going to push a good thing away.

He walked with her to his Jeep. For all the years he'd had the vehicle, he hadn't allowed anyone else in it -- until her. He opened the door to Kara. A Valkyrie. A real-life warrior. She must've carried so many soldiers to Valhalla. Part of him wanted to ask questions, but the rest of him wanted to keep quiet. He wasn't keen on talking about his past, and wasn't going to make her talk unless she was ready.

She settled on the seat and waited for him to come around to the driver's side. "How long have you had this Jeep? It's fantastic. I've never seen one in such good shape. Most Jeeps have mud all over them."

"I keep it clean." He sat beside her. "I've taken it mudding, but I like to baby it. It's the first vehicle I bought after I retired." He put the Jeep in gear and drove away to the hotel. For the first time since he'd come to Eerie, and all the times he'd driven through town, he finally saw the place. The candy-colored shops, the spires and towers, the rickety buildings alongside the seemingly gilt ones. He noticed the witches walking alongside the faeries and gnomes. The centaurs appeared right out in public alongside the sirens and swamp monsters. Shifters didn't hide their animal forms. *Remarkable.*

He glanced over at Kara. She was beautiful. Scarred, sweet, and delicate, but strong. God, what she'd been through. She still held her head up and still smiled. He couldn't believe she'd trusted him.

Or that she could like him.

He'd thought his life was over when he'd come to Eerie. Just done. He was here to find his demise. Not his future.

Christ. He hadn't thought about that until now. His mind had been made up. Now it wasn't so sure. *He* wasn't sure.

"You're lost in thought," Kara said. She reached over and squeezed his thigh. "The light changed. You're going to get rear-ended if you don't go."

"Oh. Fuck." He checked the intersection, then pulled forward. He had to get his head on straight. The castle loomed in the distance. He focused on getting them to the hotel. "Sorry, I wasn't paying attention to my driving."

She squeezed his thigh again. "It's okay."

He made the turn into the interior parking area and stopped in the same spot he'd been using for the last few visits. He parked and turned off the Jeep. "Are you laughing at me?"

"No." She snickered, then covered her mouth with her hand. "I'm not. It's just that no one's ever been so confused with me. They all know what they're up against."

"I don't?" Truth be told, he had no idea. "I know you."

"Do you?" She left the vehicle and darted around to his side. She opened the door for him. "How about instead of guessing you know, you come inside with me and show me how well you cook? I haven't had a decent meal in a long time."

"A decent one?" He left his seat, then shut the door. "I can read a recipe. I don't know if I'm that fantastic." He offered his hand.

"I don't either, but I'm willing to give you a try." She walked with him into the hotel. Within a few minutes, they were upstairs in his suite.

He blew out a long breath as he closed the door. She was with him. At the hotel. He'd offered to cook for her, but now he wasn't sure what to do. "Who are you running from?" He shouldn't have asked, but he did.

She kicked off her shoes, then wrestled out of her jacket. "You believe I'm a Valkyrie?"

"I do." He wanted to see her in her regalia -- or did she even have any? Crap. Why was he thinking about it? Would she be beautiful in her armor? Did she have armor?

"You look odd." She tilted her head. "What are you thinking? About my past?"

"It's none of my business." He had to busy himself with cooking -- anything. Shit. What was he going to serve? He darted into the kitchen and checked the stocks he'd built up after stopping at the store. The small freezer on top of the fridge held chicken nuggets and fries. Not the kind of thing to serve a goddess.

He nearly swallowed his tongue. She was beautiful, but she wasn't a goddess. She was a warrior.

Kara joined him in the kitchenette. "You have questions?"

"Do I?" God, he sounded ridiculous. But he couldn't think straight. "I do."

"Okay." She tucked her legs under her as she sat. "You asked about what I'm running from. I'll tell you -- but only while you cook."

"Chicken nuggets and fries?" He hated the way that sounded.

"I don't mind." She smiled. "It's a feast compared to ramen noodles and canned tuna."

Not hardly, but he'd do the best he could. He pulled a pan from the cabinet, then added foil. He hadn't thought the suite would be so fully stocked, but he appreciated the attention to detail. He placed the chunks of meat and fries on the pan, then turned on the small oven.

When he turned to Kara, she watched him intently. Her smile warmed him to his core. He held onto the counter. "If you want to speak, I'm listening, but if you don't, that's okay."

She laced her fingers together. "I don't talk about this often."

He understood that. His past was too damn

depressing. He waited for the oven to heat and watched her but said nothing.

"Being a Valkyrie is an honor. I love what I do, even when I have to visit the most destructive moments. I see warriors at their worst. They're dying, obviously, and scared. Every time I'm called to that final moment, I pray Odin will allow them to pass peacefully, despite the devastating situation, and that they'll find solace. I've seen bodies blown apart, limbs missing, senses gone, blood all over. It amazes me the many ways humans can destroy each other. The ways they manage to obliterate and vaporize living things. The cruelty is staggering."

He got that, too. Despite being on the sidelines, so to speak, and not being directly on the planes flying over the battlefields, he still saw some horrific things.

"I've stomached so much gore, and I'm getting tired of it. I needed a break," she said. "But this is my mission. I'm not meant to pair up or settle down. I should be off right now delivering someone to Valhalla to live in the majesty and glory of forever with Odin."

"But you're not." He put the pan in the oven and set the timer on the display.

"Nope." She shrugged. "I'm not. Because I need a break. I loved my job, but I don't love it any longer. I don't want to see anyone else blown to bits."

"I can understand that." He'd said those words so much lately.

"That's not the only thing, though." She seemed to pull into herself. Her knuckles tightened. "I wasn't lying when I said I was running from someone. I am."

"Are you in danger?" His sixth sense kicked into overdrive. He had to protect her.

"Not right now." She reached out to him and offered a shaky hand. "Helgi will hurt me, but he can't find me right now."

"He can't?" He caressed the back of her hand. "Husband? Boyfriend?"

"Ex." She snorted and held tight to his fingers. "He'd love to be my boyfriend once again."

He'd heard of being friendly with exes but had never seen it in action.

"But I'm not like other Valkyries. Most of us have a lifespan and live them. It's a long one unless one is killed. Some are. Some who are killed have the chance to come back. We're sort of immortal beings, and it's complicated."

He'd guess so. He frowned. "So, this Helgi? He's immortal, too?"

"Yes. Like me."

He stared at her. She was immortal, too? He so needed to learn more about Valkyries. "Oh."

"It's a lot to take in." She didn't let go of him. "I told you'd I'd been out for fifteen years, but I've never really been out. I just went last night to take warriors to Valhalla, but Helgi found me."

His blood chilled. "So, what you told me was a lie?"

"Not exactly." Fear filled her eyes. "I didn't mean to tell you a fib. I wanted to tell you who and what I am, but I was scared. What if you were an incarnation of Helgi? What if you wanted to hurt me? Kill me? Use my magic? I've been running scared for years."

He had to slow down. She wasn't just afraid of him. There was a lot more at play here. So, she'd told a fib. He'd lied by omission a thousand times.

"How do I know you're not dangerous? Huh?" she asked. "I saw you and I knew my mission was to help you, but I'm worried. I don't want to get hurt."

"Hurt?" He'd never. "Kara."

"I've told you so much. The truth." She bowed her head. "No wonder I'm not a great Valkyrie. My heart is in it too deeply."

"That's not a bad thing." He fought the urge to push her away like he'd pushed everyone else. Instead, he bridged the gap between them. "A good soldier cares. Some are detached, but they care. There's nothing wrong with having your heart in your work."

"No?" Tears welled in her eyes. "I'm not supposed to show emotion. I'm a warrior. I kick ass." A drop slipped down her cheek. "But you manage to destroy my defenses."

"I do?" He inched even closer. "You do the same for me."

Her lips parted, but she said nothing.

"I'm not ready to open up all the way, but I'm not scared to do this." He tipped her chin and stared into her eyes. Now or never. He tilted his head and feathered his mouth over hers. The softness of her lips, the way she whimpered, and how she touched him told him everything he needed to know.

She just might save him after all -- once he let her in.

Consider the door open.

Chapter Five

Kara snuggled into his arms. He felt so good against her. Smelled like sin and sex, too. She loved the feel of his mouth on hers. The scrape of his whiskers against her skin, the sound of his pleasure as he kissed her, the slight crinkles at the corners of his eyes and his taste… She couldn't describe the way he tasted, but it was unique.

When he broke the kiss, he rested his forehead on hers. "Wow."

"Wow, indeed." She toyed with the short hairs at the back of his head. Such soft hair. She noticed the flecks of brown in his eyes -- not just amber flecks, but chocolate and maybe green, too. Multi-faceted, just like him. On the surface, he was simple, but the deeper she went, the more she realized he was complicated. He still hadn't told her anything, but she knew him.

"I shouldn't have kissed you," he said. "Should've let you decide if this was what you wanted."

"I do." She kept him close. "Are you worried? Do you have someone I should know about?"

"No." He half-chuckled. "Single."

"Not ready to mingle?"

"I'd love to mingle, if you're offering. I like you, Kara," he said. "You told me you're not allowed to get involved, so it's probably a pipe dream, but I'm drawn to you."

"You can be." She continued to toy with his hair. "I'm not supposed to walk away from my post, either, but that hasn't stopped me. We don't have to get married, either. We can explore each other. Find solace in each other's stories and pasts. Find sanity together."

He nodded. "I'm ready."

"I am, too."

He stroked her back, then sighed. "I should check on the food."

"Sure." She let go and watched him move. He liked her. Moreover, he sure seemed to want to be with her. Most guys wanted a hit-and-run. He struck her as more of a long-term guy. Plus, he'd kissed her. She hadn't pushed. Hadn't misread his actions. He'd initiated. She couldn't recall the last time that had happened.

No, she remembered. It'd been years. The year 1864 to be exact.

She bit back a chuckle. Alonzo had been a nice guy. He'd claimed he wanted to be with her. Then he'd decided to marry Alma. Alma had been more stable. She was prettier. Sweeter. Demure. Deferred more. She was the perfect woman. *Men*.

The moment she thought she knew men, the game changed. He'd said he loved her, but not her job. She was too forthright. Too demanding. She didn't listen enough. Wasn't trying to make him happy. He claimed he wanted to be with her, except she was called away too often.

Gods… she'd met him during a time of war. Of course she'd have to do her job! Warriors fell every day. Practically every hour. She spent at least one trip a day taking them to Valhalla. What did he expect from her? If he'd have fallen, she'd have taken him, too. So many others had.

She winced. Visions filled her mind. The blood. Terror. Destruction.

A strangled cry filled her throat. She'd never forget what she'd seen. The bodies blown to bits. The men screaming in pain and agony. The hands reaching toward her, wanting any kind of help. Fallen animals.

Dead civilians. The hatred. The anger. Fists waved at her and anyone else. The divide had been too great.

The cry swelled to a full scream.

"Hey." Eric stood before her. "Kara."

She snapped out of the memory and glanced about. She was still at the hotel with Eric. Safe. Not in the midst of gunfire. Her heart hammered. The panic in her veins was too much to handle. "Gods."

"Are you okay?" He rubbed her arms. "I'm here. You're safe and I'm listening."

He didn't try to grab her. Instead, he continued to rub her arms. The move reassured and calmed her. She gulped as she tried to regain control of herself. "Sorry."

"No, I get it." He offered her a soft smile. "It gets to me, too."

"It does?" She stared at him, a little dazed. For a moment, she'd been transported back to the wilderness of Tennessee. She could smell the powder, hear the shrieks, see the blood, and feel the rumble of the earth moving.

"You're shaking." He enfolded her in his arms. "It's okay. You're safe." He petted her hair and murmured something she couldn't understand.

She clung to him. She'd never felt this weak before. Valkyries weren't weak. They were strong and steely. Resilient. Stoic.

Her knees buckled. She held onto him as he continued to pet her hair.

"I need to sit." She wobbled. The whole memory had been too much to process. "I'm not supposed to feel like this." So off-balance and upset.

"Like what?" He sat on the floor with her, then tugged her onto his lap. "Overwhelmed?"

"Yes." She balled her hand. "I went back there."

"Down the rabbit hole?"

"Yes. It felt like the whole thing was happening all over again. I was back in Tennessee watching the factions blow the living hell out of each other in the name of war." She finally looked at him. "Does that happen to you? Do you ever get… that?"

"Yes."

His simple answer helped so much, but also surprised her a bit and reassured her, too. She sank into him. "It came on so fast."

"I could tell." He held onto her and continued to murmur.

His words, despite her not being able to make them out, sounded like a song. He helped, but also pointed out, unintentionally, her failings. "I'm supposed to be strong. Kick-ass. Take charge. No prisoners. Do the job." She sounded like a motivational poster. "All of it."

"Except feel. You're not supposed to feel," he said. "Then the feeling part creeps up on you and freaks you the fuck out."

He got it. "Yeah." She'd normally kept this at bay. Not with him.

"I know."

"You do?"

"I do." His soft smile remained. Not mocking, but sweet.

She stared into his eyes. They were kind and understanding. Sensitive. She detected the steely determination of a fighter, though. A protector. A man who would respect her, fight for her, and be loyal. The kind of man she could open her heart to.

"What?" he whispered. "You look like you're a million miles away."

"No." She was right where she needed to be.

"One day, I'll tell you about my past. You'll see we're not too different."

"We aren't." She sniffed and the scent of burning filtered through the air. "I think you need to check the food."

His eyes widened. "Oh, shit. Sorry."

She scrambled off his lap as he stood and grabbed the potholder. He pulled the pan from the oven. Smoke filled the air. The nuggets were black hunks and the fries looked like slender pieces of charcoal.

She gritted her teeth. If she hadn't gotten so into her head, the food wouldn't be ruined. She owed him something better because he'd helped her. The moment they'd shared, no matter how overwhelming for her, needed to happen.

He placed the tray on the counter on another hot pad. "Well... that's ruined."

"It is." She turned on her heel and headed over to the gigantic old rotary phone. Trust the faeries to keep the old tech. When she flipped through the folio beside the phone, she found the number for room service. She dialed the number as she held onto the receiver. A moment later, the call connected. "Hi," she said. "May I place an order?"

"You sure can," the woman said. "What room?"

She should know that. She glanced over at the paperwork to catch a number... where were the numbers? Finally, she spotted the information. "Suite Four-Oh-Eight. Eric." She wasn't sure of his last name. Then again, they hadn't gotten that far.

"Ah, yes. The shifter. What'll you have?" the woman asked. "I'm ready when you are, unless you can send a bubble down."

"No. I don't have that power." She'd seen the

faeries communicate through bubbles, but she didn't possess that kind of magic. She paused a moment. Shifter? She hadn't detected that at all. But he hadn't shown any shifter tendencies. No, he had animal instincts. Most warriors did. She wondered if he knew... Of course, he knew. He'd come to Eerie. He probably knew of his abilities but had to work so hard to keep them hidden he hadn't bothered to tell her about them. That had to be it.

"Ma'am?" the woman asked.

She'd forgotten all about being on the phone. "What's on the menu?" Composure would be good right now. "What's the special?"

"We can whip up pretty much whatever you'd like. Anything sound good?" the woman asked. "Shifter might want meat. What's your poison?"

She sighed. Her *poison*? She shook her head. "How about two steaks? Medium with a vegetable and a bottle of blush wine?"

"You want bread of some sort with that?"

She gritted her teeth. Normally, she only ordered for herself. "Sure."

"I'll have it up within the hour. Probably closer to forty-five minutes. I'll bring it up myself," the woman said. "Expect Paisley."

"I will. Thank you. Don't put it on his bill. I'll pay for it when I come down later. I can give you my card if you'd like."

"No. I'll get it upon checkout. Thank you." With that, Paisley hung up.

Well, okay. She put the receiver on the cradle. When she turned, Eric stood in the doorway.

"What's wrong?" he asked. "I tried to scrape the nugs down, but they're toast."

"Smelled like it." She hooked her fingers in her

belt loops. "I ordered room service. Should be up in forty-five minutes. Steak, veggies and bread, plus wine." A groan bubbled in her throat. Ordering wine might not have been a good idea. If he had an addictive personality, he might not imbibe.

"Sounds good." He remained in the doorway. "You're resourceful."

"I have to be." She didn't cross the expanse to him. "I didn't consider you might not want booze."

"I don't struggle with that. My struggle is depression. I knew too many guys who did and saw how it destroyed lives. I tried tattooing, but once was enough. Mostly I cope by traveling and being lost." He folded his arms. "You?"

"I keep working. That's my coping mechanism." She had so much more she wanted to ask. "Want to find something to watch? Listen to music?"

"Shower with me?"

She stared at him. A bit forward, but she didn't mind. "You want that?"

"Why not? We'd be clean for dinner and have a good time in the process." He grinned. "You don't have to."

She wanted to ask about him being a shifter, but not right now. "Last one to the bathroom is a rotten egg." She removed her shirt, then bounded into the bathroom. After turning on the shower faucet, she struggled out of her jeans and shoes.

"No fair." He joined her in the bathroom and wrestled free of his clothes.

When she stepped into the shower, he followed right behind. She turned around into a solid wall of man. Gods, she'd never seen so much muscle. Correction. She'd seen it plenty of times, but not like this. He had a tattoo of a plane on his forearm. She didn't know anything about planes, but it looked fairly detailed. She stood under the water and trailed her fingers over his chest, then down his arm. The droplets added to his attractiveness. Her mouth watered. She wanted to touch him all over.

"Hi." He circled her wrist with his fingers. "Feel free to play to your heart's delight."

She held onto him. Gods, the man was strong. He had so much muscle. She wanted to touch him everywhere.

"You like what you see?" He slipped under the second showerhead. "I'm enjoying the view myself."

She'd been so engrossed in looking at him, she'd forgotten she was nude. "Oh." She feigned courage. The scars on her body weren't pretty. Some men were afraid of them and how she'd earned them. She slid her hands over her stomach to hide the marks.

"Don't." Eric stilled her. "You don't need to cover them up."

"It's okay." She'd gotten used to being shunned except within the Valkyrie community.

"We've all got scars -- inside and out -- and we don't want anyone to see them, but the vulnerability in showing them is power." He eased his arms around her, tucking her to his chest. Without another word, he kissed her.

She opened to him, and he sucked on her tongue. Electricity shot through her. Normally, she was so afraid to be vulnerable. The fear she'd be rejected was too much. Still, she opened herself to him. The scent of him, the feel of his hands on her body, the power in his kiss and the taste of him were too much to handle. It was also all too much to stop. The more she sucked on his tongue in return, the sparks increased.

She caressed his shoulders, then slid her hands

down his chest to his abs. His cock prodded her lower belly. She circled her fingers around his shaft. When she did, he growled into the kiss.

He liked it? She wasn't being too bold? She stroked him and was rewarded with another groan.

He broke the kiss. "My God." He closed his eyes, arched into her touch and sighed. "More."

Nice. She pressed her mouth to his shoulder and kissed down to his pecs. She couldn't contain the sizzles. She stroked faster, losing herself in the thrill of pleasing him. He bucked his hips. The move prompted her to suck on his nipple.

He threaded his fingers into her hair and guided her. He held her to his chest.

She loved the sprinkle of hairs on his chest. He had just enough to be sexy and not go overboard. Plus, she still hadn't gotten over all that muscle. He had a few scars she could see. Now she understood why he felt like a kindred soul. He was.

He tugged on her hair. "I need to be inside you. Fuck, I can't wait."

She let go of his nipple with a *pop*. "Then do it." The whole situation wasn't conventionally romantic, but it was exactly how she wanted it to go. Not every girl needed pink glittery hearts to be happy. She wanted her warrior.

She needed someone who was strong and independent. Someone who could keep up with her. Protect her. Love her. Could he? She certainly hoped so, but the desire to be with him wasn't the only driving force. She'd started falling in love.

So much for being solitary and unattached. Maybe she hadn't nabbed him off the street -- he'd stolen her heart. She'd been taken by the soldier.

Chapter Six

Eric let go of her hair. He'd never wanted anything more than to be inside her. It'd take every ounce of his restraint to keep from going too fast. He slipped one arm around her waist and held her tight to his chest. When she whimpered, he picked her up and pinned her between his body and the wall. He slid inside her in one swift move, not bothering with finesse. He'd never been good at suave. Why, when pushing in this case was more beneficial to everyone?

She seemed to like it. She draped her arms around his shoulders and whimpered again. "Yes."

So hot and tight. Perfect. He couldn't breathe. He needed to thrust but was too happy staying put. Wasn't that fucked up? He wanted to stay inside her forever. Her silken heat was more than enough.

She panted. "More."

"How much more?" He looked into her eyes. There, he saw the myriad colors of her irises -- blue and green with a smattering of amber flakes. Thick lashes and fires deep in those eyes. He could see forever there.

"Eric," she murmured.

Hearing her say his name was all he needed. Her voice spurred him on. The fire within him licked at his nerve endings. He pumped his hips, sliding deep into her before nearly pulling out. Within minutes he'd built into a steady rhythm.

She dug her nails in and moaned.

The second she hooked her legs around him and squeezed, he swore his brain misfired. He didn't feel the water on his shoulders. Just her fingers scraping at his skin. Didn't feel the heat from the steam. No, the temperature had spiked without water involved.

Holding her, feeling her ripple around him, hearing her sigh… It was all too much.

"I'm close," she murmured. She pressed her forehead to his. "Oh Gods." She pinched her brow tight and closed her eyes.

"Like that?" He sure did. He'd also never be the same. Not when every synapse was centered on her. He moaned, slamming into her. Would he hurt her with the ferocity of his lovemaking? Hell, he'd never been this ferocious during sex. She brought that out in him.

"Come for me," she said and opened her eyes. "Come with me." She bucked and ground on him.

"Can't hold back?" He wasn't even sure how he'd been able to form rational thoughts, let alone say complete sentences.

"No." She moaned again. "I need to come." She tensed as he continued to pump. A shiver rocked through her.

He lost himself in the feral desire to claim her. To be with her. The climax started low in his belly, then spiraled through his veins. Just a few more thrusts and he tipped right over the edge.

"Yes." She clawed at him, then collapsed against him.

He pumped his hips a few more times as the orgasm rocked through him. As the trembling subsided, he rested his forehead on hers and panted.

She continued to cling to him. "I can't stand."

Her laugh echoed in his ears. "No?"

"My knees won't hold me up."

He wasn't sure how long his would, either. He managed to set her on her feet but kept his arm around her. "Let me wash you."

"A gentleman." She offered a lazy smile. "You

wear me out."

"I doubt that." He grabbed the washcloth with one hand and kept his other arm around her.

Kara took the cloth from him and lathered it before giving it back.

"Thank you." He kept holding her while he washed her. Sliding the cloth over her belly, breasts, hips, arms and down to her legs. Every inch of her was beautiful. The scars, the hills and valleys of her, even the tattoo on her upper hip. He didn't want to let her go.

"Should I rinse?" she asked.

"You should." He had to clear his head. He'd only ever been this tangled up one other time. This was different, though. He wasn't in a high stress situation, and she wasn't going to leave him for another man.

Without a word, she washed him. The motion of her hands on his body, the swipe of the cloth and the suds sliding down his chest were all too much to handle. He groaned as he rinsed. Holy hell.

She switched off the water. "May I dry you?"

She didn't have to ask. "Only if I can dry you."

"You may." She blushed from her hairline to her chest. "Listen to us. So formal."

He grabbed a towel from the rack and dried her. Once he finished, he wrapped the towel around her. "Doesn't matter. I like it."

"I do, too." She tucked in the towel and helped him wipe the water from his body. She swept her gaze over him. "You work out, don't you?"

"As much as I don't like it, I do." He stepped out of the stall and paused. He could have sworn he'd heard something in the other room. A prowler? Someone trying to hurt them? He held up his hand.

She said nothing and held still.

He crept over to the door and cracked it, then peeked out into the other room. A woman with flame-red hair pushed the cart just inside the main door before exiting. His stomach flip-flopped. Food? His hands trembled as he backed away from the door.

Kara peeked around him. "I ordered room service. I thought I told you, but maybe I didn't. I'm sorry."

"You did and I forgot." He hated the unsettled feeling. Hated the shaking, too.

"I got steaks." She blushed again. "Ordering that was too forward, wasn't it?"

"No. Just had me on edge." He tucked the towel around his hips and left the bathroom. He headed into the bedroom to retrieve a shirt and pair of shorts.

"I can tell." She touched his bare shoulder, and the sparks shot from his arm to his heart. "I knew it was safe," she said. "I can feel it."

"Can you?" What an odd thing for her to say, but an equally odd thing for him to think. He'd believed he had a sixth sense about his surroundings. "Valkyrie training?"

"Sort of. It helps because then I know to go out on a journey, and I won't get killed. It's still dangerous to go, but I won't end up dead, either."

He admired her. There was so much more to her than anyone could see. Plus, she was damn sexy.

"Was it too forward to order food?" she asked.

"You're fine." His embarrassment won out. "I should let my guard down more often." Even if it went against every cell in his body to do so.

"No, you should be you." Her skin glistened as she stood there in the towel. She was beautiful and vulnerable.

He stared at her, letting her words sink in. He

wasn't sure he could be vulnerable ever again. Was it even possible? He'd had his heart stomped on too many times, as well. Plus, that day never would leave his mind.

"You do need to understand not everyone is out to get you," she said. "But that'll take a lot of time."

"Will it?" He didn't move. "You're not out to get me?"

She smiled -- not mocking, but sympathizing. "No." She chuckled. "I came here without my armor or a change of clothes. No one knows where I am, and I don't care. Something in me knew I'd be safe here. I trust you."

He didn't speak right away. "You don't trust often, do you?" Maybe not at all. He dropped his towel, freeing himself to be vulnerable with her. He offered her the shirt. "Here."

"You don't like me *au naturel*?" Her sly grin lit up her face. "I don't like to eat in the buff, though. So, thank you."

"I'd lick you clean." God. He'd said that. It sounded so dirty and dorky.

"I'd love it." She dropped her own towel before donning the shirt. "Thank you."

"Yes." His stomach growled. Then he was famished. He should be -- fucking her in the shower had worn him out. He dressed in his shorts. "You said something about steak and 'taters."

"I did. The faerie said it was good for shifters." She froze. "Oh shit."

"What?" He hadn't caught on right away. "Huh?"

"I said something I shouldn't have." She darted away from him to the other room.

"About?" He joined her at the table as she

opened the lids on the plates. "I don't understand."

She sank onto the chair across from him. Defeat clouded in her eyes and voice. "The faerie who took the order called you a shifter. I didn't ask, but she said it and the information has been stuck in my brain ever since. You hadn't said anything and it wasn't mine to bring up." She scrubbed her forehead with the back of her hand. "I messed up. You didn't want to tell and I forced it."

"You didn't." He wasn't sure how to reassure her. "It's okay."

"That I revealed your big secret? I'm going to pay for it." She buried her head in her hands and said something he couldn't understand around the muffling.

He'd bet she could kick serious ass during a journey and could be scary as hell in battle, but she still had a tender side. "You didn't do anything wrong."

"How?" She groaned. "The elder will be pissed. We're not permitted to out anyone."

"Let her be upset. You haven't done anything wrong." He reached across the table to her. "I didn't know, so it's not a secret of mine. How can I have a secret if I didn't even know? It's a mess, but it's not yours to clean up. It's just a mess, plain and simple. Don't worry about it." Christ. He was a shifter? That had to be impossible. "Maybe she meant the wrong person. Maybe she made a mistake."

"I doubt that."

"Are you sure?"

"How are you not sure?" she asked. "You're in town. You can't come to town if you're not para, so it must be true."

"I got lucky?" He shrugged. "They felt sorry for me? I don't know, but I'm not magical. I have no powers, and I can't do anything special. I'm just a soldier." He caressed her hand.

"You have skills. Animal instincts." She stared at him. "Don't you?"

"I guess." He'd never thought about it. "I did the job. Whatever was asked of me to keep my guys in check, I did it."

"Only guys?"

"On the last tour, yes." He sighed. "Suffice it to say, I wasn't special."

"You are." She offered a feeble smile. "Some shifters don't shift. They possess the qualities of shifters without actually changing form. Keen instincts, finely tuned senses, just no fur or whatever."

"I had a good sense of smell -- you've got to know where the fuel is coming from and if it's turned or flowing when you can't see it. The vapors." In his line of work, leaks were deadly.

"Do you have good reflexes?"

"Decent." He shrugged again. "We should eat before this gets cold."

"Oh." She shook her head. "I guess I ruined everything."

"No." He squeezed her hand. "You can't ruin what's not known. I'd wondered why I've been drawn here. Why I keep coming back to Eerie." He'd thought it was because of something bigger than himself, but what? He hadn't been sure. Maybe it was her. Anything was possible.

He let go and cut into his steak. "How do you know where you come from? I was raised by neighbors and wouldn't know where to start researching my family."

She smashed her potato and added sour cream. "I'm not sure. I know where I come from, so I never considered needing to research."

"Think the nosy faerie would know?" She knew everything else. He wasn't keen on talking to her, but he had to try. With her abilities, she probably had all the answers he needed. "I'd like you to go with me." He wasn't doing this alone.

She toyed with the steamed carrots. "I'd like that."

"Then it's settled." He didn't need to know his entire lineage right now. Not even this week or this month. He'd rather get to know her. He had a lot to talk to her about and he was dying to tell her. The words needed to come out. He'd tired of hiding it and keeping quiet.

He'd been a good soldier. He'd kept the secrets, but he wasn't in the service any longer. The secrets didn't hold power over him. His past wasn't important. Not to his present.

He ate in silence and watched her. She hadn't brought up the faerie, but he'd detected a bit of jealousy. Kara was tough, yet tender and graceful. Kickass, but sweet. He wanted more than a thousand days with her. A thousand nights wouldn't be enough, either. Hell, he wanted forever.

She smiled as she finished her steak. "That was delish."

"It was." He'd spoken more about the view than the food. He pushed his plate away and stretched. The move wasn't the sexiest thing to do, but he didn't care. "How long until Helgi finds you?" The question had been on his mind since she'd mentioned him before.

She tucked her knees to her chest and nibbled on a slice of the bread. "Hard to say. He could be on my scent right now. Could've lost me."

Helgi had lost her, all right. She might not be

Eric's woman, but he refused to let her go to the bully. "Think he did?"

"No." She tensed. "He senses me."

"Ah." That was fucked up.

"The longer he goes between finding me and the more separation through body and soul jumping, the lesser the chance he should know me."

"But that hasn't always been the case?"

"No."

He nodded once. "What if you have someone?"

She frowned. "What do you mean?"

"What if you're off the market?"

Her frown deepened. "Huh?"

"What if you and I are a couple? Can he still attack you if you're with someone?"

She shook her head. "Not really."

"Then that's what we'll do." He'd made his mind up, but he'd wait for her. If she had doubts, he'd give her space.

"That'd work, but there are issues," she replied. "Lots of issues."

She'd mentioned there might be roadblocks. "Do you want to?" He had the impression she liked him. "Tell me why this won't work."

"Do I want to stay single? No."

"Okay." He could work with that.

"But I'm supposed to be with him."

This time, he sighed. The fear was winning out. She wasn't interested in Helgi. Hell, she was scared of him. "I get that you've got to find him, but you're hesitant. You don't want to find him. Not really, do you?"

"No, I don't."

"Then this is your chance to break the cycle. You and me." He offered his hand. "We find a way to make this work. We can. You don't have to be with him. You deserve better and to be your own person."

"I can?" Her eyes widened and she paled. "And be a Valkyrie?"

"Sure. I want you to be you -- not a version of you from the past or the version of you someone else wants you to be. You be you." It was a simple answer, but hard to put into action, he knew all too well.

Fire lit in her eyes, and she grinned. "No one's ever said that to me before."

"That you should be yourself?" He snorted. She'd been hanging around the wrong people. "I'm not like other men. I know who I am and who I want. You're the one I want. I like when you're being yourself."

Her grin spread across her face. "I'd like that, too."

"No hiding or being someone you're not. You're free with me." He reached for her again. "Promise."

"I accept that." She unfolded her legs and let go of him, then rounded the table. She straddled his lap. "I very much accept."

"Good." He curled his fingers under her chin. "I have a big bed and room for more than me. Share with me?" He wanted to ask her to share more than that, but he held himself in check. Pushiness was for another day. Right now, he just wanted her -- to be safe, happy, and in his arms.

"I'd love that." She kissed him. "So much."

"So would I."

Chapter Seven

Kara snuggled against him. Once upon a time, she'd been romantic. The little gestures, the kisses and touches... it all made her day. She lived for long mornings in bed, holding the man she loved. Being together. Being young. The gifts, the caresses, making love all night long. It was all so magical and sweet. All so tender and uncomplicated. If she could've bottled those moments, she would've.

Then she went to war. Year after year of war. Year after year of going into dangerous spaces to retrieve the brave.

Then Helgi. The danger of being with him. The anger. The screaming. The chasing and abuse. Every time he found her, he'd romanced her, only to try to kill her to "protect their love." What kind of love was that? If the target of one's love had to be killed to be protected, then it wasn't really love.

Then she'd died the first time. The second time. The third. It never got easier.

Somehow sweet romance didn't work. She wasn't into BDSM, though she applauded anyone who was, but sweetness didn't set the beat of her heart thundering. Why should it? Love wasn't real. But Eric was. He had her thinking second thoughts. Not like other men.

She kissed him again. "Why do I feel so safe with you?"

"Because I won't take advantage." He patted her ass. "Come to bed."

"Yours?" Where he'd invited her before? "Yes, please." She didn't need to sound so eager, but she didn't care.

"Then welcome to my bed." He kept her in his

arms and carried her to the bedroom, placed her on the bed.

She liked the white walls. Or were they cream? She wasn't sure. She'd never been in the hotel as a guest. Not in any capacity. She'd lived in Eerie for this round of her life and the elders didn't want her or the other Valkyrie to hang out in the hotel.

Why not? The place was warm, inviting, and Eric was there. That was plenty of reason for her.

The softness and fresh scent enveloped her. This was comfort. No one wanted anything from her. She doubted she'd be able to keep her eyes open. It was barely seven in the evening, but she'd spent too many nights not sleeping. Too much time interrupted. She half-expected to be pressed into duty. Why not? She wasn't ever not on the clock.

She crawled between the sheets with him. The bed smelled nice, but he smelled even better. Sin and sex. Clean, but dirty. Heat swirled in her body, and she tangled up with him. Cream slicked across her pussy lips. If he touched her, she'd combust. Being with him was the best.

He switched off the light. The remaining sun filtered through the curtains and stretched across the room. She hadn't noticed much of it. All she knew was his arm around her.

"When you go on a mission, what is it like?" he asked. "I guess I should ask if you don't mind me asking you that before I blurt it out."

"My missions?" No one had ever asked her about them. They hadn't asked for permission to talk about it, either. This was genuine interest.

"If you don't mind, I'd like to know." He turned her face to his. "I like to look into your eyes when we talk. You've got beautiful eyes."

"So do you." She slid her arm across his waist, but hesitated. Her missions, as he called them, weren't that exciting.

"How do you know when to go?" he asked.

She should be on her guard. These were nosy questions, but he'd been to war. He'd been in tumultuous places. He'd seen hell. "I get the call like a trumpet. Some of the Valkyrie hear a hunting horn. Mine sounds like the brass version. When the sound comes, I'm expected to drop whatever I'm doing and go. Sometimes, I'm already there and it's a matter of fighting alongside the warriors if needed. Other times, I simply go to them. It's never pretty."

Talking about the biggest part of her life wasn't her favorite thing to do. It took a lot out of her.

"I'm sure it's not pretty." He caressed her arm. "I'm sure it's demoralizing and can be disgusting."

"It's what humans do to each other in the name of their side." She shrugged, trying to minimize the situation. What she'd seen wasn't minimal. It was devastation. Tragedy. Destruction. Yet, she tried to make something beautiful come out of it.

"I've seen what humans do. Awful things."

"I bet you have." She shuddered. Imagining his past bothered her. It didn't scare her, but it made her skin crawl. He'd seen so much. He hadn't even told her about it yet.

"Do you have to stay where it's dangerous? You said you fight alongside. Are you able to go?" he asked. "Are you seen?"

He wanted to know so many things. For once, she wasn't afraid to talk. "I am seen. I get the call that I should be there and follow the sound. When I arrive, I never know where I'm going. I'm simply drawn to the warrior and go where I'm needed. The person is dying, and I need to help them make that final journey. I kneel with the warrior and reassure them. As they fade, I wrap my arms and wings around them. They die in my embrace and I spirit them to Valhalla." She didn't usually like discussing this much, but he made unburdening herself easy.

"Do you talk to them?"

"I do." She stared at him and trailed her fingers over his cheek. The stubble under her fingertips tickled. "I wrap my wings around them, reassure them they're being rewarded, and carry them away."

"That's honorable." A slight smile curled on his lips. "Invaluable."

"It's my job." She hadn't felt honorable in a long time. Would she ever again? Doubtful.

"It is." He kissed her. "And it takes a strong will to do what you do."

"It's who I am," she said, minimizing her role once again. Every cell in her body screamed to laud her job. She had a mission, and she insisted on doing it properly. But time had dulled her zeal.

"And I like who you are."

He liked her? It was still too hard to understand. She snuggled up to him, though. "Why are you so good to me? You don't need to be."

"No?" He kissed her temple. "You deserve good in your life."

"And you're willing to be that good?" She wanted him to be there. Wanted him for a long time.

"I am," he said. "Why don't you like the front desk faerie? I don't even know her name."

She didn't want to answer him. The mess was too great. "No reason."

"Really?" He crinkled his brow. "Want to be honest? I can tell you're not being truthful. You're dying to talk about it. You've told me so many other things."

He had a point. She had to shore up her courage for this. Talking about her job or the shit she'd seen was one thing, but explaining her displeasure with the faerie was another.

"You don't have to." He caressed her cheek. "I pushed too hard and it's none of my business."

"No." He was right. Part of her didn't want to talk about this at all, but more of her wanted to get the story out. To see if someone else believed her. To know that someone had heard her. Everyone seemed to believe the faerie. Maybe the other woman wasn't bad, but the situation wasn't great. "Five years ago, I thought I might have found someone who could really love me. Someone who wasn't... him. I started falling hard for the man, but before it got too involved, I caught him with the faerie. She claimed she didn't know he and I were seeing each other and once she found out, she backed off -- for a while."

"That was nice of her."

"Maybe," she said. "But she knows things. She knew what she was doing, and she continued to do it. Then she blamed me for the problems. She has that ability to read souls. I don't like it because it gives her the upper hand. It wouldn't be so bad if she used it for something positive, but she weaponizes it."

"I know she does." He sighed and trailed his fingers down her bare arm. "I know she's not innocent. She knows what she's got and what the ability can do."

He knew? She paused a moment. Maybe he did believe her. She cleared her throat and kept going. If she lingered too long considering the situation, she'd never get the story out.

"It turned out she knew he wasn't single and

didn't care," she said. "She wanted him, so why not take him? If he'd let her, then she was going to do it. He'd been interested in her, so they should be together. I lost respect for her. I get that some people stray, and things aren't always meant to be, but that doesn't mean you get involved or intentionally cause problems and make it about you. Wait your turn, you know?"

"I do."

"You do?"

"When I first got here, she let me know she knew my information, and it was sad that she was stuck working at the desk." He half-shrugged. "I didn't feel bad. I felt awkward, honestly. I didn't know why she was telling me everything she knew. It wasn't my business."

"She likes to talk." She wasn't surprised the faerie talked so much. For all she knew, it was the faerie flirting with the single man. Why not have any man who came along? It hadn't stopped her before.

He frowned. "How'd you find out?"

"About her? I asked her." She'd never forget it. "I asked and she told. No remorse. Just flat determination. She likes men, all men, and wants as many as she can have. I don't blame her for wanting to sample far and wide. I mean, I don't have that kind of determination, but if you do, then go for it. Just go for men who aren't already involved."

"You're right."

She shook her head. "I thought it was my fault. There was something wrong with me, that's why he strayed. If I was someone else, anyone else, maybe he'd have stuck around. Maybe he wouldn't have given in to her. I'm too toughened up, too hard. That's why he cheated."

"There's nothing wrong with you."

She shook her head again. "There are a lot of things wrong with me. I leave too much, I work too hard, and I have a messy past. I try too hard to please people, and I have my own mind. I don't follow directions that aren't the Valkyrie way. That's a huge issue. It's too much for men to handle."

"Maybe some men, but not all," he replied. "Anyone with honor won't give up. Not that easily."

His simple words confused her. "No?" The question came out choked. She'd been told plenty of times by the other Valkyrie that there wasn't anything wrong with her, but she hadn't believed them. They gave each other pep talks all the time. This was different. He had no reason to lie to her, other than he wanted her to stay in his bed. "You're joking."

"No." He gathered her close. "You're a good, sweet woman. You deserve someone who will love you, too."

"Love?" That was a foreign concept. Even with Helgi, she hadn't been in love. She'd been in lust. Wrapped up in a crazy determination to have someone. Love wasn't something that happened to her. "I don't know that it exists."

"I know it does."

No hesitation. She snorted. It couldn't be true. She'd never met anyone like him. "Are you certain?"

"I am. I see it in your eyes. It's in your actions, too. Taking those warriors to Valhalla is a labor of love. Yes, it's your mission, but no matter how jaded you get, you keep doing it because you love it. You know that journey needs to be done and those warriors need you to take them. You help them know they're not alone. It's tender and sweet, while being fierce and determined."

His words amazed her. She couldn't believe him.

"Eric."

"It's true. It might be labor, but it's one of love. It's one you believe in."

She nodded as the words continued to wash over her. "Like you and your guys."

"Yes." Something flicked in his eyes. "It is."

She wasn't sure what she knew, but she'd touched a nerve. Instead of pressing, she let it go. "You're right. I want them to be treasured. They gave all."

"They did," he murmured.

"You did, too." She caressed his chest. "You're my warrior."

His eyes flashed. "I am?"

"Yes." He was all she wanted. "But the need and desire I have for you are the reasons I'm scared."

"Of?"

"You getting close to the faerie." She hated admitting that. "It scares me because I worry you'll decide she's better or she'll turn your head because she can. I wasn't enough for the other man, wasn't enough for Helgi and what if that holds true with you? What if I'm not enough? I probably won't be." Gods. She'd said that all out loud.

"You're afraid you'll be left behind," he whispered.

"Yes."

"I'm not Helgi."

She froze. She hadn't expected him to say that.

"You've been loved and left so often you're convinced everyone will leave you, because your job is dangerous or because that other woman claims she's more interesting," he said. "That's what this is about. You're having a hard time believing in yourself."

"Yes." Shame washed over her. She shouldn't let

the worry get to her like this. Love wasn't a big deal. Being left wasn't a big deal. It happened. If love wasn't going to happen, then it wasn't. She couldn't change that.

"I told you I'm not like other men. When I make a decision, I stick to it. Second thoughts and indecision don't help. Usually, it gets tricky and causes someone to get hurt. Maybe even killed. I chose to go on this journey, and I'm not changing my mind."

The reassurance and trust in his eyes shimmered. She believed him. Most men wouldn't have those feelings and would've run. Not him. "You chose me."

"I did and do."

She shouldn't be so exhausted, but the conversation had worn her out. She had what she wanted. The entirety of the day and the confession were too much. She needed a break. There was a nearly naked man beside her, but she wasn't in the mood to fuck him. She'd rather be held right now. Would rather be loved. She'd never felt that way before.

"It'll be okay." He stroked her hair. "You've had a lot thrown at you. You deserve time to process."

"I am tired." She closed her eyes. "I appreciate you, and I want to keep spending all these moments with you. I want so much from this. From us."

"But you can't keep your eyes open?" He kissed her forehead. "Sweetheart, I'll be here as long as you need me. I've got you."

"I've got you, too." She could rest now. She'd found a safe harbor. She could be herself and might even have love -- for the very first time.

For once she actually believed she deserved love, too.

Hot damn.

Chapter Eight

Eric held Kara while she slept. The fact he had her thrilled him. The excitement of having found her, a kindred spirit. She was everything he'd ever wanted, and he needed to memorize everything about her. Every inch of her body, every part of her mind. He wanted to hold her forever.

He also wanted to open up to her. The fear of doing so kept winning out. After the things she'd said and the ways she'd peeled back her own layers, he knew she'd understand. So why was it so difficult to talk to her?

He didn't want to face his past. It was too disturbing. He kept hearing Sadler's voice. "*You're not at fault. We couldn't do anything.*"

He knew logically it made sense. But his sense of duty didn't agree. He'd let people down. Men were dead. Cal was gone. It wasn't fair. He couldn't change a thing about it.

"Eric." Kara sat up. "I have to go." She scrambled out of bed. No dressing. Instead, she shivered and switched forms. Glittering gold armor covered her arms, legs, and chest. Leather and fur accents added to the design. Fur boots covered her feet, and her hair shook loose with beads and braids within the wild tresses. She was beautiful and dangerous. She transfixed him.

She met his gaze. "I'll find you." She tipped her head back and donned a glittering gold helmet featuring tight gold horns. A spear and shield appeared in her hands. She nodded once, then disappeared.

He sat up, not concerned at all that she'd find him. She'd come back. "You will." He nodded. A piece of his heart went with her. She was heading into battle. Not a battle against her, but she was in danger nonetheless. He was worried about her. She could get killed. Could get hurt. Maimed. Might not be able to return to him.

His heart lodged in his throat. Now he understood the way Harleigh had felt. Every time he'd gone on tour, she'd feared he wouldn't come home. At least early on, that's how she'd felt. She'd claimed he had a death wish. He wanted to die. He'd never wanted to end his life and wasn't going into dangerous situations to harm himself. He had a job and was there to serve.

She didn't like his career. She'd liked the uniform, but the actual job was too much. The attention she got from being connected to someone in the military seemed to please her. People checked on her. She got special treatment. Then there were the condolences because he was gone. But she hadn't been happy. The attention only lasted so long. After a while, she'd been just another woman left behind.

For him, she hadn't been just another woman. She mattered. She hadn't seen that. She wanted a man who worked a normal, nine-to-five job.

He stared at the ceiling. When he'd left on the last two tours, Harleigh hadn't written and only called a couple times. She wanted kids, but that wasn't possible when he was halfway around the world. He'd tried to give her what she wanted. Tried so damn hard.

Then she met Mike. Mike was the perfect guy. Had a steady day-shift job, was involved in her life, smart, and everything she claimed she'd ever wanted. He was her future, not Eric.

Then she got pregnant. Eric knew damn well the timing was off. He'd come home in May and the baby was born in October. The little girl hadn't been born early, either.

He sighed. At least Harleigh told him the truth before the baby had been born. The little girl was Mike's, and he wanted to take custody.

The truth helped, but it hurt like hell. He'd thought he could still be with her and wanted to raise the baby. Might not be his, but he'd be what the kid needed -- a father. He might have even left the service for them, but she'd left him too fast so he'd stayed in.

Probably just as well. He wondered if she was happy. Harleigh loved to laugh and travel. He'd wanted to bring her along with him on his various tours, but it wasn't always possible. He sighed. The little girl had to be about thirteen by now. Was Harleigh still married to Mike? Or had she cheated on him, too? Part of him cared, but most of him didn't. He had to move on regardless. Life hadn't stopped and he'd still been required to go on tour.

He shook his head. Enough with the past. He turned his thoughts to Kara and wondered where she'd been sent. Was she safe? The place had to be dangerous, but if he fixated on that he'd drive himself to the brink.

Trust the mission, trust the good, and do the job.

When he'd been a young airman, he'd totally bought into that line of thinking. No, he'd bought into it the whole time. Still did. But he'd seen so much damage. So much tragedy. Christ. Why did people have to treat each other like shit? The destruction wore him out.

He glanced over at the clock. The yellow-green numbers illuminated the room. He'd slept until two a.m.! Well, hell. Having her there must've been his cure for sleeplessness. Unfortunately, she wasn't there now.

And he couldn't sleep. Once again, he was damn tired and his insomnia was taking over. When he closed his eyes, he saw that day. Saw the wreckage. He heard the screams. The nightmares always returned. He'd never be free. He might as well leave the bed and wear his body out so he could collapse later. He had no other choice.

Before he'd retired, the commanding officer told him to take leave. Just go anywhere and sleep. Fat chance. Sleep hated him with a bloody passion.

He further debated getting up or staying put. He could drift off, but it wouldn't be good sleep. If he moved, he'd be exhausted. He practically lived with exhaustion. Why not keep up the trend? Wandering and reading would take his mind off worrying about Kara.

He left the bed and switched from his shorts to a pair of boxers and proper shorts, plus a T-shirt and pair of socks. Once he stepped into his sneakers, he grabbed the swipe card, plus his phone, and left the hotel room.

He paused outside the door as it closed. She could come back and wonder where he'd gone. Or the job might take a while. Some of his missions were longer than expected. Though, some went faster than they should've.

He groaned. Next time he'd ask about the process. For now, he needed to roam. He went down to the atrium. The bright lights were too much contrast. He blinked past the brightness.

"Hi." The faerie rounded the corner. "You're up early. Can't sleep? Or just excited to be in a castle? I love castles. Working here is a dream. I love it and can't imagine being anywhere else. It's so much fun. But we're talking about you. How are you?"

He wondered if she ever took a breath. "I'm fine."

"You seem upset." She cocked her head. "I never introduced myself. I'm Tasia."

"Hi."

She grinned and her wings fluttered. Bright red veins stuck out in her wings, and they seemed to glow. Or was that glitter? He wasn't sure. Her hair brightened as well. "You're Eric," she said. "And you're worried. You're tense."

"I am." On all three accounts.

She cocked her head again and stared at him. "Nope. There's something wrong. Who upset you? No, I know. The Valkyrie left you. She walked away, didn't she? She does that. She gets involved with people, then leaves them high and dry. She did that to a friend of mine. It sucked because she broke his heart."

"Whoa." He held up his hands. "I'm sure I don't need all that information. It's not mine to know."

"Oh. I guess not." She frowned. "Why, then, are you out at two thirty in the morning? Do you need to prowl? You need to walk? I know shifters need to roam. That's it. You're just wanting to wear off some energy?"

"Stop." He backed up. "You don't know her."

"I know enough," she said. "I know you're a shifter who can't shift. You're freaked because you've never considered being a shifter. You're upset that I insulted your friend, even if it's proven that she's not who you think. It's too much." She rested her hand on her hip and her wings fluttered even more. She narrowed her eyes. The smug tone of her voice annoyed him.

"You do know a lot." He didn't want to talk to her, but she'd know so many other things. She could direct him to his past, which would be nice if she wasn't such a talker or had to be so judgmental. She didn't have proper justification for her thoughts.

"I know her well. Did she tell you about our connection? About him?" she asked.

"She did."

"That I stole him?" She waggled her head. "Huh?"

"She mentioned something about you talking."

"Oh?" She rolled her eyes and shook her head. "We talked. I accused her of ignoring him."

"You knew they were together, though," he pointed out. "And you knew he belonged to her, so to speak. You knew and still made a point of doing it."

"So?"

"You could've kept your hands to yourself. Could get the true story before you do something sneaky. Yeah? People like to lie. They cheat, they lie and do really shitty things to each other. You don't have to encourage it. You could be better."

She crinkled her nose. "I could've."

"Keep that in mind. There are always two sides. The truth you see might have been okay from your point of view, but did you consider hers?" he asked. "You never thought about anyone but you."

"Why should I?"

He wanted to roll his eyes. She was so cranky and combative. Did she know she'd overstepped? He'd bet so. "Because it's the civil thing to do. Think about others." He paused to give her time to understand. "Look, if you don't want it done to you, then don't do it to others."

"But…"

"I get it. You've been hurt. Haven't we all? But we all need to think about each other more. If you don't like something, then neither would she." God, he sounded like the counseling sessions he'd had to help with all the time when he was in the service. "You know?"

She crinkled her nose again and sniffed. "I do." She sighed. "So... What... Never mind."

"What? You can ask." If it was within reason.

"What do you see in her?"

A loaded question. "She's funny, sweet, fierce, and we have a lot in common. She gets me." So much more than most.

"Oh." She sighed and folded her arms again. "You're down here, though. Did she leave you?"

"She went on a mission."

"She does that a lot." She shrugged. "She disappears. You won't know when she'll be back."

"She's a Valkyrie. That's part of what she's meant to do." He paused again. "Have you ever asked her about it?"

"No."

"It's who she is."

"I suppose you're right." She frowned again. "You're searching for something."

"I am." He wanted her help yet didn't. Still, he should ask. "I want to know where I came from. Who I came from. I'm here in Eerie, so I'm para. You say I'm a shifter. That explains why I'm able to be in Eerie, but how come no one's ever told me? How come no one ever mentioned me being a shifter?"

"Easy." She shrugged. "Your father was adopted."

He nearly toppled over. Holy shit. "He was?"

"He was. Your grandparents were from here and were shifters, but only half. You can find information on them in the scrolls."

He didn't understand. "Scrolls?"

"The Hall of Records. Haven't you ever heard of that?"

"No." He'd have to ask Kara about it and see if she'd go with him. He assumed she would. At least he hoped so. He wanted to share this with her. "Okay."

"Your grandparents were both half-shifters. Half human and half bobcat. They could shift, but they feared that your father, who had the abilities of the bobcat but couldn't shift, would be hunted or used. To keep him safe, they put him up for adoption and lied about his lineage."

He needed a few moments to process this. How did she manage to know so much? "You can read all that from me? In my mind? From my thoughts?"

"I can."

"You're in my mind?" He didn't like that and hoped she could read his discomfort.

"I'm not in your mind, but I can read your overall... presence." She shrugged, then sighed. "I told you it gets me into trouble."

"Why don't you use that ability for good? Instead of maybe not something so good, you know? Work for the Hall of Records and help people find their pasts. That'd be good for you. You could use your talents."

She stared at him. Her eyes widened and her jaw went slack. She said nothing right away. "Are you serious?"

"I am. You've helped me." He had to corroborate the information, but still. He had a start. "Why not? It'd be good for you."

She grinned. Her wings shimmered brighter red and her glow increased. She was pretty, but not his type. His girl was out being a super badass. He admired Kara but could encourage the faerie. Maybe he'd help Tasia do something with herself other than driving wedges between others.

"You're a great guy. I'm glad you're staying here." She threw her arms around his shoulder and hugged him. "The best. I can't wait to tell you how it goes."

Awkward. He wasn't a hugger and didn't like being touched without permission. "Okay. Let go." He tried to get loose. "I'm not a great guy. I just had a decent suggestion."

"You did." Her grin turned wicked. The gleam in her eye unnerved him. "Very good."

The tone of her voice bothered him. "Stop."

She crooked her brow. "I made my point." She turned on her heel and walked away.

A streak of electricity ran the length of his spine, but it wasn't the same one as with Kara. This one made the hairs on the back of his neck stand on end. He glanced over his shoulder to see Kara behind him.

Kara remained in her gold and furs. Her wings were open as if she'd just landed and her hair was a bit out of place. Red infused her cheeks. He wanted to say something clever but feared even opening his mouth. He hadn't done anything wrong or let her down, but things didn't look good. Anger blazed in her eyes. Anger and something he couldn't discern.

"Kara." He hated the defeated sound of his own voice. He couldn't make anyone happy.

"You were supposed to be different," she said, and her form switched back to the T-shirt and bare legs. "Supposed to be."

"I am." He wasn't the kind to screw her over, but he had to explain -- and fast.

Chapter Nine

Kara watched Eric. She knew what she'd seen when she'd arrived. The situation was all too familiar -- the guy in her life connected to the faerie. Was the rotten woman trying to take him? She would have sworn Eric wasn't that kind of man, but this didn't look good.

She tucked her wings away. Her first instinct was to get angry and get even, but that wouldn't help. It'd drive a wedge between her and Eric.

She stared at him, waiting for a reply, but she hadn't asked a question. Right now, she wasn't sure what to say.

"Can we talk?" He offered his hand. "Please?"

That wasn't a bad idea. Besides, she doubted he asked for things like this too often. She wasn't wearing shoes. Why hadn't she changed before she switched forms? Then she would've been able to return wearing the same outfit. She didn't have socks, panties... a bra. Nothing. "Let's talk."

"Come here." He crossed the expanse to her. "I'll carry you."

"I can walk." She'd do it. No one had to cover for her.

"You're not going barefoot on this floor. I have no idea when they cleaned it last." He turned around. "On my back. I've got you."

She draped her arms around his shoulders as he hoisted her against his back. He threaded his arms beneath her legs.

"There we go." He patted her shin. "Ready?"

"Sure." He smelled good and felt even better. Still, her heart ached. He could be about to destroy her. She glanced over at the peripheral. A man stood in the shadows. Helgi?

She dug her fingers into Eric's chest. Helgi couldn't be there. It wasn't possible. He couldn't have found her. She'd been careful. Hadn't she?

"What?" Eric stepped into the elevator and didn't put her down. Wasn't she getting heavy?

"What's wrong?" he asked. "Sweetheart?"

"Nothing." She forced her eyes shut and turned her head until the doors pinged. The second she heard the bell she opened her eyes.

"You're full of shit. Besides me, what's upset you?" He caught her gaze in the reflection on the mirrored wall. "Talk to me."

"Not here." She tried not to shiver. If Helgi had found her, he'd try to attack. Time hadn't made him more amorous. It'd made him more dangerous and angrier. It made him chase her.

Somewhere within him, the original Helgi might still be there. Might still love her. He might also have died over the centuries, replaced by the detached version. The version chasing her seemed more removed and had become a monster.

The doors opened and she half-expected to see Helgi there. She shivered again, until she noticed the empty corridor.

"We're safe." He rushed to the suite, then set her down long enough to open the main door.

She darted in first, needing to get the hell out of the hallway. He stopped her and held up his hand. When she paused, he motioned for her to stay put. She froze. If he felt the need to check the suite, then he'd sensed her fear. Was it his shifter sense? Or just good training?

"We're safe." He nodded. "It's clear."

She blew out a ragged breath before collapsing

on the sofa arm. "Gods. I thought I saw someone watching us."

"He scared you."

"He did." As much as he could. Why wouldn't he? Helgi had power and liked to use it.

"He does that often?"

"It all depends. If he can find a way to jump into a new body, then the soul goes on, but it deteriorates who he was and the changes aren't always pleasant." She rubbed her bare arms. "He's not the same man."

Eric sat on the coffee table and faced her. "I get it. I made it worse, didn't I?"

"No." She wasn't sure how to explain. "Everyone makes it worse, but it's no one's fault."

"That's not good enough." He sighed, then offered his hand. "I admire you."

"You do?" She allowed him to grasp her fingers.

"I do. A lot." He stroked the back of her hand across her knuckles. "You put yourself in danger without question. You do the job."

"I try." She wasn't always successful.

"Your mission was half the reason I was up tonight."

That thought chilled her. She nearly jumped to conclusions but held herself in check. "Oh?" She had to keep calm. There might be a perfectly logical explanation.

His gaze never left hers. "I don't sleep much. The past gets in my head, and it's hard to close my eyes. Tonight, I was worried something would happen to you and I got edgy. I needed to move around and wanted to walk. Eerie isn't that bad after dark. Not as bad as some of the places I've been on tour."

"Not usually." She wouldn't suggest going to the gnome encampment or the section of town where the dwarves lived. They weren't the best areas for midnight walks.

"I left to walk myself to exhaustion, but before I got out of the atrium, Tasia stopped me."

She never wanted to hear the faerie's name ever again.

"We talked." He squeezed her fingers. "Sweetheart, I defended you."

"I'm sure you did." She tried to contain her irritation, but it wasn't easy.

"Hold up," he said. "What have I told you?"

"You're not like other men," she said flatly.

"I'm not. She came on to me, dragged you through the mud, and I didn't bite. I didn't want to bite. I tried, instead, to educate her." He curled his fingers under her chin. "I chose you. No matter how hard she tries, I'm not interested in her. She knew she'd done you wrong, and I held her to it. I tried to get her to change her ways, but I doubt it worked. You and she are like oil and water."

That all sounded plausible and correct. "I know."

"She's only happy when she has the upper hand -- or at least when she believes she has it. You're not bothered by having power. You don't seem to want it, but she does. That indifference on your part drives her harder to upset you. I've seen it a thousand times."

"Have you?" She didn't doubt him, but that didn't make this easier.

An edgy look crossed his face. "Can we go into the other room? I want to talk to you, but I need to hold you. Please, will you? I need you to understand."

"I do." She remembered what the elder had said. Her ultimate mission was to help the warrior to Valhalla. He wasn't dying, but he needed her and she'd be there for him. She stood and held out her hand. Once she tugged him to his feet, she led him to the bedroom.

He disrobed completely and crawled onto the bed.

Kara hesitated a moment, then followed suit. Nude, she joined him and stretched out on the mattress. "What do you need to discuss?"

He moved the sheets aside and settled on his back. She curled against his side as he put his arm around her. "I know you're a Valkyrie. I understand what you do. You take warriors to Heaven."

"Valhalla."

"Right."

"You're not dying," she whispered. "Promise."

"Maybe not, but something within me is broken."

She wanted to say no, but instead let him talk.

"If you're here to help me cross over, then so be it. I don't know if I'm ready to go, but I'll do what's asked. I'm tired, frustrated and scared. The nightmares are killing me," he said. "So, if it's my time, then it's my time."

"Eric." She held him tightly, not sure how to reassure him.

"Ten years ago, I was in Jordan for the third time. Volunteer. We were supporting a campaign and providing refueling services. Most of the time, things were safe. We did the job and didn't worry much. That Thursday was different. There was something in the air. At the time, I didn't know what was wrong, but I could feel it. We filled the trucks like normal and drove across the tarmac to fill the planes. As we fueled the largest aircraft, something exploded. Fuel is combustible, but no one was smoking and we'd followed regs. Still, there's always the chance it could be dangerous. This was different, though. Townes had said something to me right before the explosion. We'd been laughing about a stupid joke, then parts of him were missing, and we'd both been thrown across the tarmac. He was on fire, then he was gone."

"Oh no." No wonder he had nightmares. He'd seen hell up close.

"Insurgents had infiltrated the area and set charges on the tarmac. I don't know how they did it and never asked. All I know is that they weren't detected. I guess they were planted underground somehow."

"Eric." She held him even tighter, wishing she could make the bad memories go away. He'd seen unimaginable horror.

"The truck exploded. Everything was on fire." His voice came out choked. "I was close enough to be thrown, but not end up in flames. I'll never forget seeing Townes or the screams. I couldn't have changed anything and can't help feeling responsibility. We did what we needed to do, but he shouldn't have died."

"No, he shouldn't have." She stroked his chest. "I wasn't the Valkyrie who took him to Valhalla, but he's there."

"Of course, he is. He's a hero. I'm not." He shook his head and a tear slipped down his temple. "I could've done more. Should've been more vigilant. I'm no hero and never should've been given those damn medals."

"Slow down."

"You should go to another warrior. I'm just a guy who served and watched his friend get torched."

"No." She'd never dealt with this part of the cycle before. She'd never saved anyone. Today, that changed. He needed to be saved and she'd do it. He deserved to go to Valhalla with a clear mind and the battle in his head eased. She crawled onto his chest and straddled him.

"Kara? I'm dying, aren't I?" More tears slipped down his temples. "I should've died when Townes did."

"No." She dragged him upright to her chest. She hugged him as he cried. She cried along with him. So what if the other Valkyries saw her? She and Eric had to get the anger and sadness out. Bottling it up wasn't healthy for anyone. She couldn't imagine how he'd kept himself contained all this time.

"I should've died too," he screamed, but held onto her.

She stroked his hair. "No."

"Why?"

"You had a job to do. The mission isn't over, even if it feels like it is. Far from it," she murmured. "You have more to do. You were meant to come to Eerie, to me."

"To die?"

"To live." She cupped his jaw in both hands. "We've both seen hell. Both have been damaged. But we also needed to find each other. Find kindred spirits. We've both fought battles for so long, and it's time we stopped fighting them. We give over our burdens to each other and rest."

"How?"

She offered him a soft smile. "You've showed me there is good in this world. There's good in people, even when it seems like there isn't. You proved to me that opening up is the way to let go. You've been the one to save me."

He slowly met her gaze and said nothing right away. "I did?"

"You did." She continued to pet his hair. "I've never talked to anyone about my past or my missions. Then you come along and I tell you everything. That's pretty big."

"I suppose it is," he whispered.

"And I doubt you've talked about what you've gone through. You probably haven't uttered the name of your friend in years." She rested her forehead on his. "And it's been killing you. You don't have to keep that inside. You're safe to talk about it with me."

He didn't speak for a long time. "Kara."

"I knew when you came to Eerie because I was tasked with helping you. Not to cross over, although you've earned your place in Valhalla. I'm here to give you your sense of peace back. I wasn't there, but I know the Valkyrie who was." She stayed close to him. Her breasts grazed his chest. "I know it's hard to understand, but he was at peace."

"How do you know?"

"My elder was the one who helped him." She wasn't sure why she knew this, but she did. Maybe it was the elder speaking through her. Maybe it was just that innate sense. Didn't matter, really. "I'll take you to her in the morning."

"You will?"

She nodded. "And I'll prove to you that the story you won't accept is true. You weren't at fault, and there wasn't anything anyone could do. He's at peace."

He narrowed his eyes as he seemed to consider what she'd said. Slowly, he nodded. "I believe you."

She'd hoped he might, but she hadn't been sure. "I'm here to help you find peace, and you will."

He caressed her back. "You'll stick around?"

"As long as I can." She hadn't thought about the chance she might not be able to stay with him. She'd been promised to Helgi years ago, but she didn't love him. Maybe she never had. What she did have was strong feelings for Eric.

"I'm holding you to it."

The sincerity in his eyes spoke to her soul. She never wanted this moment to end. Ever.

"I've never been this open with anyone before. Never talked about Townes to anyone not part of that day. I locked it in my heart, never to think about it again, but you pulled it out of me. You made it easier to get out." He kissed her. "Thank you."

"My honor and pleasure." She needed to be closer to him. Wanted him moving inside her. In her soul. "Make love to me."

"Yes." He said nothing else as he kissed her. He situated her on his lap. His erection slid between her slick pussy lips.

She groaned into the connection and shifted on his thighs. As she did, the blunt head of his cock nudged the mouth of her cunt. Just a little more and he'd be inside her. She wriggled until she slid onto his shaft. The fullness overwhelmed her. She gasped and dug her nails into his shoulders.

He broke the kiss. "Fuck."

She nodded. She had no words, not now. Instead, she rode him. She lost herself in the sheer pleasure of being with Eric. He understood her in ways she wasn't even ready to comprehend. Each time she settled to the root of his cock, she cried out. This wouldn't last long. She needed him too much.

Eric took control of the act and bounced her on his lap. He kissed her with abandon, sucking on her tongue. He threaded his fingers into her hair, tugging lightly and drawing a yelp from within her. The pain spread through her body and morphed into pleasure.

Her nipples beaded, and electricity shot through her skin.

"Eric," she murmured. "Gods."

Eric moved faster, pulling her harder onto his cock.

Her mind buzzed. She wasn't sure what to think and didn't care. She savored every second. He made her fly. Made her forget her job, her past. Made her want to give up her job and stay right here with him.

He was the first man she'd ever felt those feelings for, and it wasn't bad. Sure, she wasn't positive she'd fallen in love, but she knew this connection was different. He wasn't like everyone else.

She rode him with feral need. Nothing else mattered.

"My God. Kara." He held onto her backside as he nudged her onto her back. He crawled over her, never losing a beat and continued to thrust.

Her thoughts completely scattered as the orgasm washed over her. She held on tight and embraced the climax. "Eric!"

"That's right, sweetheart. Scream for me." He kissed along her jaw and down her throat. "More. Let me know you need this."

"Eric," she cried out. She wasn't able to make her words legible. The coil wound tight within her snapped as she came. The shudder rocked through her. For a few moments, she simply floated on the good feelings.

"Love hearing you say my name." He pistoned into her. "Mine."

She loved when he said that. Her heart did belong to him. She held on as he surged in her to the hilt and came. His cock throbbed and his breath tickled her cheeks.

"My knees are weak." He propped himself on his forearms and knees over her. "You did that." Perspiration glittered on his skin and a bead slid down his temple.

"Did I?" She kept her arms around his shoulders. "I'm glad." She'd worked him hard and felt the benefits of his hard body. She wanted more from him. A lot more.

"I am, too." He kissed the tip of her nose. "Don't go."

"Not sure I can. My knees aren't working, either." She toyed with the hairs on the back of his head. "I don't want to go anywhere."

"You don't have to." He rolled onto his back with her in his arms and against his chest. "Can't imagine being anywhere else."

"Me, either." She'd found her version of Valhalla on earth and wasn't about to lose it. Not for anyone or anything. Eric was her future.

Her warrior.

Chapter Ten

Eric woke later that morning with Kara beside him. He grinned. He'd been the luckiest man alive to find her. Or she'd found him. Didn't matter. She made him happy. He chuckled softly to himself. He'd slept. For the first time in years, he'd slept -- and well. No tossing and turning. No nightmares. Just slumber. And he felt refreshed! He couldn't remember the last time he'd felt this way. Because of her? Had to be. Thank God.

She stirred and opened her eyes. "Hi."

"Hi." He grinned. "You're a miracle worker."

"Am I?" She brushed her hair from her face. "How's that?"

"I slept." She probably didn't see the monumental win in his statement, but it was true.

"Good." Kara smiled. "What time is it?"

"After ten." He'd gotten at least six hours of sleep. Hot damn. "I want to take you to dinner today."

"We can." She stretched. "If I don't get called on a mission, that would be nice." The sheet slid low on her body, showcasing her breasts. Her nipples beaded.

He stared at her tits. She had beautiful tits. The kind a man could get lost in and never want out. He slid his palm over her smooth belly to her ribs. "I want to show you off. I'm proud to have you as my girl." That might be overstepping, but last night, he'd declared she was his.

"I like that." Her smile increased in wattage. "Your girl."

"You are."

"You're my warrior." She caressed his cheek. "We should get up, though. I need to check in with the elder. She'll have information for you."

"The faerie did give me some details, but I'd like the ones from the elder more. What's her name?"

"Brynhildr. She's nice, but stern. She'll be irritated I'm not single, but I've always been the troublemaker." She shrugged. "Helgi got me into a lot of trouble."

"I don't want to cause issues, but I like us being an 'us'." He traced the lower swell of her breast with the tip of his finger. "You know she knew what happened?"

"I do." She sat up. "She'll be glad to talk to you. We never get to touch base with the living once we help someone move on. It's sort of a one-way journey."

"I'm sure." He watched her leave the bed. "I should've offered to have your clothes cleaned. I might have a shirt you can borrow, so you don't have to do the walk of shame in the clothes you arrived in."

She shrugged again. "I don't mind. No one really looks at me." She crooked her brow. "Would you believe most beings are afraid of me? They see a Valkyrie coming and think they're going to die. Those who knew me with Helgi run the other way because they know he's lurking."

"Still?" He didn't like that. He wanted her to be able to live freely.

"He will until he's moved on to another body or finds another object of his affection." She donned her panties and bra. "He'll move on eventually, unless he's neutralized."

"What if he was? Would you be able to breathe? Relax?" He had to know.

"Yes." She tugged her shirt over her head, then fluffed out her hair. "It'll happen one day."

Maybe sooner than she knew. He'd give his life for her. It was too soon and he didn't care. He wanted her to relax and be safe. "Will Bryn…"

"Brynhildr," she replied. "What about her?"

"Will she be okay with meeting me? I mean, will she not see me as a threat?" He shoved the bedding out of the way and left the bed. He strode over to his bag and withdrew a pair of boxers. He'd nearly run out of clean clothes.

Then again, now that he'd found her, he wanted to stay in Eerie. That meant moving. Why not? If he was from the town, he might as well find a place and put down actual roots. He'd been mobile for more than half of his life. He could have a home with her. Roots. Permanence.

Love. He'd wanted that for most of his life.

"You're stuck in your head." She strolled over to him, nearly dressed, but with bare feet. "You okay?"

"I'm good." He threaded his arms around her. "Better than okay. I was thinking about the future. Thinking about what I want to do and how I want to do it."

"Oh?" She tipped her head and draped her arms about his shoulders. "Good things?"

"Very good. I want to move here. Live here."

"In the hotel?"

"Eerie," he said and patted her butt. "With you."

"Me?" Her eyes gleamed. "You know how to flatter a girl and get what you want."

"I flatter the girl I want in my life." He squeezed her backside. "We'll figure it out eventually."

"We will."

He swore she glowed. "Now, about visiting the elder… What do we do?"

"Oh." She nodded. "You get dressed, then I'll take you to the safe house where we first met. It's our home base of sorts. She's there."

"Is there a dress code?"

She blinked. "No. Why?"

"She's an elder. High up in the ranks. It's a sign of respect to dress well in her presence? A courtesy?"

"I guess you're right. We don't really have ranks, though. We're all on the same level. She's just older."

He donned his shirt and jeans. "You refer to her as the elder. It's a sign of respect." He put on his socks and shoes, then grabbed his phone and key to the room. "Do I need my car key?"

"You don't need the key." She tucked her hands into her back pockets. "We respect each other. It's kind of lateral."

"Are we walking?" He slipped his key into his duffel, then zipped it.

"Nope." She pulled a small mirror from her pocket. "We can use a portal."

"Oh?" Portals? He'd learned so much in a short time and had a thousand questions. Where had she gotten that little mirror? He hadn't seen it in her jeans, or even the outline of it in her pocket. "How doers it work?"

"Like this." She held the mirror in her hand. "Home base." She flicked her fingers as the mirror opened a shaft of light. The image in the light cleared. "If I'd had this that night, I might never have met you."

"Is that a dorm?" he asked and stood beside her. "Where is it?"

"The house. It's pretty much a dorm." She gestured to him to join her as she stepped into the light.

He'd never done this before, but he might as well try something new. He moved into the light, but it was more like stepping into a new world. The room was dark, bland and a little boring. "Huh."

"What?" She stood beside him. "What'd you expect?"

"A castle or fortress. I don't know." He chuckled. "It's ordinary."

"Utilitarian, but also unassuming. If an enemy can't find us, then they can't hurt us."

"Who would want to argue with a Valkyrie?" The whole situation amazed him.

"Helgi."

"Fair." He hated to think about the asshole.

"Or other beings who want us to die. We have some magic and anyone who wants it bad enough will kill to get that magic." She strode over to the door. "Bryn?"

"Downstairs," called a voice. "Kara? You're safe?"

She grasped his hand and rushed to the lower floor. "Not only am I safe, but I'm happy." She burst into the room. "Bryn?"

The sheer ordinariness of the room shocked him. She hadn't been kidding about the place being boring. An older woman with blonde hair, graying at the temples, sat on a stool at what appeared to be a highboy table. She turned a moment after they entered the space. "Kara. I wondered… You're the warrior."

The tips of his ears burned. He wasn't used to feeling this embarrassed. This was like meeting his girlfriend's parents back when he was in high school. "Hi."

"Bryn, this is Eric, the warrior. Eric, this is Bryn, the elder." Kara beamed. "Bryn, he's got lots of questions for you I know you're suited to answer."

His heart hammered. Now he was nervous. What had he screwed up? Had he said something wrong? "Hi."

Bryn stood. She was taller than he'd expected. Impressive. "Hello," she said, her voice flat. She swept her gaze over him. "You make Kara happy."

She spoke like Kara wasn't even there. "I hope so. She makes me happy." He slipped his arm around her. "I'm damn proud I met her. She saved me."

"I know she did." Bryn nodded. "Kara?"

Kara let go of Eric. She stood tall and notched her chin. "I hear it." She switched from her street look to her full Valkyrie form. When she spread her wings, the room darkened.

He nodded to her.

"I'll find you," Kara said. She disappeared in seconds, leaving him with Brynhildr.

"She'll be safe." He sighed. "I worry about her."

"You do?"

He turned his attention to the elder. "I do."

"She can handle herself." She gestured to the other stool. "Sit."

He complied. "Thank you."

"You wish to know about that day."

He gulped. She was so businesslike and flat. "I thought you didn't get emotionally involved?" He regretted being pushy, but Townes deserved better.

"Who says I don't?" She didn't flinch. "You forget I do this all the time. Every day I bring someone to Valhalla. It's more frequent as time marches on."

"It is?"

"Humans destroy each other in more dangerous and vile ways. More than before and it's more effective." She laced her hands together. "It's not easy to see it."

"No." He'd witnessed enough.

"My heart hardened after many years. It thawed a bit but cooled again. You, though, managed to melt

Kara's heart, and I'm glad. She's been alone a long time." She narrowed her eyes. "You bring out the good in her."

"I'm trying." He liked the compliment.

"She brings the life out in you."

"She does." He thanked God she did.

"You need to be smart with her. She's been hurt many times and needs love and understanding."

There was wisdom in her words. Odd, but still wisdom. She reminded him of the hardened commanding officers he'd known. "I will." He treasured Kara.

"I know you will. I can see it in your eyes. You enjoy her and are an equal." She relaxed. "You asked about that day. Are you sure you want to know?"

"I did want to know." He'd wondered when she'd get around to talking. "You don't have to tell me."

"You need to know."

He nodded. He'd like the truth.

"Townes came from a long line of warriors. Not every member of his family, but that's his line. He knew when he'd joined up he risked losing his life. He never blinked," she said. "But you know that."

Townes was a devoted airman. He followed the rules, was affable and quick with a joke and helping hand. He was smart, too. "Yes, I do."

"He knew you'd come from a line of warriors as well." She dipped her head. "I bet you didn't know that."

"I have family who served." He had the photos.

"You did -- in the Revolutionary War, Civil War, in the wars in Europe... with the Vikings." She paused. "You didn't know you have Viking blood, did you?"

"No." How odd. He'd had no idea. "I never

traced my line."

"I suppose not." She crossed her ankles. "Townes knew that day he'd be walking into danger. You did, too. Your shifter abilities helped you to sense it. So did your old, old magic. Viking warriors did certainly, as you put it, kick ass, but they also had magic. Yours comes out in your senses, and the shifter blood enhances it."

He'd had no idea about that, either.

"You both knew there was something wrong, but he knew there was nothing anyone could do to change it."

"He said there was no reason to be upset."

"He believed it."

"He said that all the time." Like a mantra.

"He didn't know how he'd pass, but he'd felt it coming. When that bomb went off, he accepted what happened."

"He was calm." Or they'd all been so deep in shock it felt calm.

"He was because he'd accepted it," she said. "I came to him as he lay dying. No one saw me because I was a blur."

That made sense. There was a lot of confusion, so lots of things went unnoticed.

"Before I spirited him away, he asked me to protect you and help you move on. You were a good friend and he cared. He didn't think of himself -- he thought of his crew and you."

He nearly fell over. "Really?"

"He knew you were special." She frowned. "Didn't you ever wonder why you were spared and were barely physically hurt when others died?"

"Every day." His scars were internal. "I never got over it."

"I'm sure you didn't," she said. "You've been traumatized, but you did make it -- which wasn't an accident. You were meant to keep his memory alive, meant to keep living and showing others how to move forward."

She'd stricken him dumb. None of this made sense but was completely believable.

"When I came to him, he wasn't scared. He had no secrets and was at peace. He went happily." She paused. "Did you know he was miserable?"

"His girl had left him." He remembered that quite clearly.

"She did, and the depression was overtaking him."

That figured. "He wouldn't talk to anyone." He'd tried to get Townes to let some of it out, to no avail.

"Like you?"

"I wanted him to open up to me." He'd thought he could help him. "He was my best friend."

"He was. He tried to talk, but the words were stuck. He trusted you but got lost in his own head. When he crossed into Valhalla, he found peace."

"Did he suffer?" He needed to know.

"No. The soul left while the body perished."

He needed time to process what he'd learned. There was so much to take in. He blinked back tears. His head swam with all the information.

"Now it's your turn -- you help Kara. She's depending on you." Brynhildr stared at him. "If you like her, then you'll make her job easier. You'll make her existence better. You can both help people now while you take a break. You both need rest -- but if you're not able to accept her job, you need to say that now. Don't lead her on."

"But my abilities? You understand them?"

"Answer my query first. Do you understand her job? Accept it?"

"I do." That wasn't in question. He wanted to challenge her, but he kept in check.

"I understand your abilities. You're a shifter who can't shift and never will. You're a good man with the senses of a bobcat. Use those and your big heart. You and Kara will be unstoppable."

"But my past…" He sounded so whiny and it annoyed him, but he didn't want to let anyone down.

"You know it. Go to the scrolls, but you know it." She pointed to his chest. "In here. The people who raised you were your parents. The ones who protected you are, too. You've always known them. Remember the Lewises?"

"The neighbors, yeah." They were close friends of his folks.

"You felt close to them."

"I did." So what?

"Because they are your aunt and uncle."

Holy fuck. His life made so much more sense now. They were involved in his life, knew so much, and were invited over all the time… because they cared. They were mentoring people and kept an eye on him -- so they could ensure he wouldn't forget his family. He saw them in a new light. Everyone was trying to protect and help him. "They encouraged me to join the service."

"Because they knew."

"They did," he murmured.

"Feel a little more complete?" She smiled and left the stool. "You felt it, but never really were. You just needed guidance."

He nodded. "I did." Realization hit hard. "Now I'll help Kara. She needs me. She's fierce and independent, but I love her and hope she'll want me, too."

"She does and I knew you'd feel that way." She winked. "Keep Helgi at bay and seal that union."

"I will." As long as Kara would let him, he would. He'd do the best he could for the woman he'd come to love.

Chapter Eleven

Kara stood at the gates of Valhalla and watched a soldier she'd helped off a battlefield move on to his final reward. Pride welled in her. She'd helped him. She'd gotten him to where he needed to be. She'd done that, and the whole thing felt rewarding. She was honored to be the one to do it.

He glanced back and grinned, then stepped into the light.

Once he disappeared, she headed back to her home base. As much as she wanted to help the soldier, she wanted to get back to Eric and home. She missed him.

Maybe they'd only been around each other for two days, but they were destined for a lifetime together. Those hours were long and wonderful, even if they were stressful, too.

She'd waited so long for him, though. Too long. Now that she had him, she wanted a million more days with him.

She flew home, but her thoughts turned to Eric. They needed time to just be together. Be dorky, silly, sleepy, cuddly… all the couple-y things. Watch movies, dinner together, something goofy at the bar… All of the above. She needed to do them with him.

He made her happy. Not just because he respected her job, but because he liked her. She mattered.

Still, they needed more time.

She landed outside the house and tucked her wings away. The powerful look worked well for transport, but her wings were cumbersome otherwise. When she went inside, she'd get a proper shower and change her clothes. She wanted to look her best.

"Going somewhere?"

She hadn't seen him, but the second she heard Helgi's voice, she froze. Panic rocked through her system. He'd found her and sounded angry. No, he sounded blue-fire pissed.

"Helgi." She kept her voice even. "You're in Eerie." She didn't bother to turn around to face him -- not when she sensed him.

"You're in Eerie. I go where my lover is." He walked around her until he stood before her. His eyes blazed. "You left me."

The Helgi she'd once known was sweet. Tender. He was a male Valkyrie and proud, but non-combative. The man before her didn't look like him, sound like him, or have the same love for her, but this man did have one thousand percent of the fury she'd come to expect. He scared her -- not that she'd show fear.

She stood tall. "I didn't."

"No?" he growled. "You ignored me."

"Can't ignore someone I didn't see." She had to keep her voice even, despite her irritation. Any show of fear would empower him.

"You saw me."

"I saw whomever you'd taken over."

He glared at her. His lip curled in a deep sneer. He clenched his fists and his chest heaved. "You belong to me."

The Helgi she'd known wasn't a monster. Tough in battle and strong, but never dangerous without reason. He had a sense of fairness. This man, though, didn't. He simply wanted vengeance. "I belong to no man."

"Not even him?" Helgi's magic ripped Eric from the house. Eric landed hard on the grass.

At least he'd been dumped on the soft lawn, not the asphalt. She focused on Helgi. As much as she wanted to protect Eric right now, he could handle himself. Besides, the best protection for both of them was keeping Helgi busy and diverting his attention.

"Tell him," Helgi demanded. "Tell him you're not his."

Eric stood and brushed himself off. "I know she's not mine. She belongs to no man."

She admired his smart and quick thinking. She turned her attention to Helgi. "What do you want from me? You don't love me. Haven't loved me in centuries. You love war and destruction. You love upheaval. Danger."

Helgi continued to glare at her. She noticed his hand on his sword. She hadn't trusted him in years and expected him to fight.

"I want my fated mate back," he snapped. "You're it."

She rolled her eyes. She wasn't afraid of him any longer. Not now. This wasn't her Helgi -- hers was gone. "You're not mine."

"And he's not your fated mate." Helgi brandished his sword and slashed it at Eric. "He's unworthy."

"Whoa, big guy." Tasia rushed up to the house. She held up her hands. "You told me I was your fated mate."

Helgi's eyes blazed. "This is a trap." He slashed at Eric again and a streak of crimson spilled across Eric's chest.

Kara's patience thinned. This wasn't how Eric's story was supposed to end. It wasn't even how their relationship did. She'd put a stop to this right now. "Helgi."

"Yeah." Tasia stepped up to him. "You're a liar."

"A liar and a monster," Kara said. She pointed the tip of her spear at his Adam's apple. "You have caused harm. As a Valkyrie, you aren't permitted to do harm. We respect life."

"I'm no longer Valkyrie," he thundered.

"Then you're no longer worthy of my respect." She pricked his throat. A speck of blood ran down his neck. "What do you have to say for yourself?"

"I say we castrate him." Tasia fired a blast of white light at him. "Save Eric. I've got him for now."

Kara hesitated for a second. Tasia was helping her?

"Go. I can't hold him forever." Tasia nodded. "Go."

She rushed to Eric and carried him into the house to Bryn. "Heal him, please." She placed him on the table.

"You know I can." Bryn nodded. "Blast Helgi. He's no Valkyrie. That's a demon."

"I knew it." She kissed Eric on the cheek. "I will come back."

He offered her a tiny smile. "Slay that demon."

She wanted to linger but didn't. He was right. She needed to slay this demon and move on with her life. She bounded outside and summoned all her Valkyrie strength.

Tasia nodded. "I get it. We need to help each other -- not steal. I'm slaying my demon, and now it's your turn." She backed off and the light dissipated.

Helgi lay on the ground in a heap. He sprawled there, dazed but not dead. Her heart ached. The man on his back wasn't the one she knew -- not the original one. This one was in someone else's body with Helgi's mangled spirit. His spirit wasn't bad, but it'd been fractured so many times. She stood over him and pointed her spear at his throat. "A Valkyrie only attacks when provoked and doesn't look for danger. We help and serve. The only one you're serving is yourself. The Helgi I know was valiant and stoic. He believed in the Valkyrie code."

"I believe you belong to me," Helgi snapped and grabbed at her.

"Wrong." She clocked him in the head, sending Helgi's spirit rushing out of the body shell.

Tasia stepped up and sent a shaft of light at the spirit form. "You can rest now." Her magic morphed him into a translucent body. "Helgi's all yours," she said to Kara.

"Just a moment." Kara blew her horn, summoning another Valkyrie.

"This is no war," the brunette Valkyrie said. "Yet it appears you've had a battle."

"A war for his soul." Kara pointed to the man. "The shell is at the end of his war."

The brunette Valkyrie covered the shell of a man in her wings. She nodded before tipping her head back. She disappeared in an instant, spiriting the warrior home to Valhalla.

Kara relaxed a fraction. Now she could handle the bigger issue.

She turned to Helgi's spirit and spoke to him. "You. I loved you so much once. For so many years. I believed you. Trusted you. Then war, time, and battles took you away. I never stopped loving the Valkyrie who fought beside me. The one who knew my body well. The one I loved. But you're not him any longer. Time and distance have changed you. It's made you hard. The Helgi I knew wasn't hardened -- not like this."

Sadness filled Helgi's eyes. "You're right. I lost myself along the way. Kill me."

"I won't." She kept her spear pointed at him. "But I banish you. Never take another body without permission. Find the one who can love you in this form. Be free." She removed her spear and screamed. The cry split the air. Tears slid down her cheeks and her heart broke. She'd seen him die so many times, but never cried over him because she knew he'd return. Not this time. She'd truly and wholly freed him. Helgi disappeared in a vapor.

Another cry ripped from her throat. She'd never felt so angry. She'd loved and lost. She'd been shortchanged. But if that hadn't happened, she wouldn't have Eric. Could he be the true love of her life?

He could. She wasn't the same starry-eyed girl who'd fallen in love with Helgi. She'd grown -- harder, stronger, and more determined. Tired. Eric had healed some of that pain. It made her want to be free and find her heart. Her passion.

Tasia touched Kara's arm. "You need to rest now."

"What?" She hadn't noticed the faerie was still there. Not since she'd separated Helgi from his body. "Sorry."

"No, I should apologize to you." Tasia let go. "I thought I understood, but I didn't. I thought I was smarter. I needed to learn. Eric is a good man. It's because he set me straight and suggested I go another direction that I turned my life around. I owe him a great deal. I owe you, as well. There is no pride or goodness in destroying someone else. You deserved better."

"We've all been scarred." There was no need to

hate any longer.

"We have, but I'm not using anyone or my scars again. I liked helping you and liked being useful. I have magic I didn't know I possessed. I want to use that magic and my gifts. I got a job at the Hall of Records so I can help more."

"Good." She didn't need to know all that, but it was fine. "I'm proud of you."

"No more chasing men -- not men who aren't available. No more cutting anyone down, either. It's not nice or helpful." Tasia clapped her hands together. "You've encouraged me to turn over a new leaf and I have. Thank you."

"You're welcome." Kara wobbled. Her knees and soul were weak. She'd been worn down by the fight. By life. She hadn't had to expend this much energy in so long. She needed to sit. "I should go inside."

"It's time to rest, Valkyrie. Let others take the load for now." Tasia directed her into the house. "Helgi's body has gone to Valhalla, while his spirit wanders the earth. In the mean time, your warrior needs you."

"Does he?" She swore she heard words coming from Tasia's mouth, but none of it made sense. She had to be that worn down. She wandered into the house. The darkness and quiet unnerved her. Where was Eric?

Brynhildr rounded the corner. "Oh, gods. You're covered in blood." She steered Kara into the living room. "We'll clean you up, but first come here with me."

She allowed the elder to lead her into the other room. She swore she was swimming. Floating? Something close to that. A form was sprawled on the sofa. Rags? Splotched with blood? Pale. Eric? Who else? She'd brought him into the house herself. "Eric?"

"Sweetheart?" Eric managed to sit up. "I knew you'd do it."

Not that she'd return, or that he'd missed her. His words were deliberate. He knew she'd do it. She'd heal the situation and come back for him. She'd be there. She switched the rest of the way from her Valkyrie form into her human one. "Eric?"

"I'm still me." He offered a weak smile. "You didn't think I'd be here?"

"I worried." She had. He could've died.

"We're connected and I'm not leaving you. I finally found you and I won't let go. Remember, I said I'm not like other men." He grinned. "More than I ever knew."

"You're not." She brushed her fingers over his cheek. "I thought I'd lost you."

He chuckled. "Apparently, being part bobcat shifter means I have the cat's nine lives." He shrugged. "Besides, I finally feel like I belong."

"You do?" She held his hand in both of hers. "You probably do have nine lives, though."

He squeezed her fingers. "We have a lifetime to sort this out. If you'll stay with me, give me time, and love me, then I'll make you feel like the luckiest girl in the world. Be my girl. Please?"

He didn't have to plead. She leaned over him and feathered a kiss to his lips. "Your Valkyrie."

"My determined, fierce, beautiful woman." He curled his fingers under her chin. "I vow to be your warrior as long as you'll have me."

"I'll have you for the rest of our lives." She couldn't wait to take the next step with him.

"We've got that lifetime to fall more in love and explore," he said. "So much more time for exploring."

"Yes." She didn't need that much time to know

she'd fallen for him. She was already in over her head and happy to be there. But exploring sounded darn good. It sounded perfect.

"Are you heading home?" Brynhildr asked. She stood in the doorway just beyond him. "You don't want to stay here, I'll assume."

"No." She helped Eric to a sitting position. "I'd like to put down some roots."

"Would you?" Brynhildr asked. "Eric?"

"I would." He slid his arm around Kara. "I'm ready for that, too. We'll figure out what we want together and find something that's just ours. I have no idea what we'll find or where, but I want to stay here in Eerie with you."

"I'd like that." She wasn't sure where they'd go or how they'd sort everything out, but she knew she had a partner. She also knew Eric would treat her as an equal. He was the man she'd been waiting for.

Could he be her fated mate? She didn't have to think about it for long. She knew. She'd found her other half.

Epilogue

Eric stood outside the throne room, and his knees nearly buckled. He'd met a real queen. Piper didn't conduct herself like royalty, but she did have a cyclops. He respected the hell out of the cyclops. That man had seen shit and was still there to talk about it. Plus, he had a kick-ass name. Diesel.

Kara inched up to him and sighed. "Wow."

"That was intense." He slipped her hand into his. "They're cool, but I felt so small."

"Diesel is a hugely tall guy." She bumped shoulders with him. "But I got to meet her with you, so that made it the best."

"It did." He'd met the queen and cyclops, but that wasn't nearly as important as getting home with Kara. They'd finally found a house in the shifter part of town and were accepted in the neighborhood. He'd even found relatives there. He hadn't expected to find any other bobcat shifters, much less to be accepted. The moment Kara saw the little house, she insisted on buying it. He wasn't going to tell her no.

"It's kind of odd to see Tasia at the Hall of Records, too." She held his hand as they walked to the Jeep. "She seems happy."

"She is." He hadn't talked to Tasia, but when they'd visited the Hall the last time, she'd been in her element showing off the scrolls. "But I don't want to talk about her."

"No?"

He opened the door for her. "I'd like to talk about you."

"You would?" She crawled into the passenger seat.

He rounded the hood and settled behind the wheel. "I would. I have a surprise for you."

"You do?" She palmed his thigh while he put the vehicle into gear. "About what?"

"I got the house paid off." He drove away from the palace. "No more payments. While you've been out working hard saving other warriors and spiriting them to Valhalla, I finished sorting out my family tree. Seems I was supposed to inherit money from the Lewis family. Enough to pay off the house."

"You did?" She squealed. "It's all ours!"

"All ours." He drove across town to the little house. He didn't notice the homes around theirs or the landscape as he drove. All he saw was her. He couldn't wait to get home. To have her in bed and taste every inch of her.

She'd done such a good job furnishing the house. Now it was all theirs. He turned onto their street, then into the driveway.

"I can't believe we own this." She rushed out of the Jeep, barely giving him time to park in the garage. "Eric, I've wanted a place to live that's not someone else's or a dorm for so long."

He eased up behind her and slid his arms around her waist. "Now you've got what you want."

"I do." She turned in his embrace. "Do you believe in fated mates?"

He'd thought about that so many times. "I believe we're put into each other's lives for a reason."

"Oh?"

He scooped her into his arms and carried her to the front porch, then placed her on her feet long enough to unlock the door. Once he had the door open, he carried her inside and didn't stop until they reached the bedroom. "I believe we're here because we were meant to find each other. You and I were meant to cross paths."

She held on tight. "Are you certain it's just cross paths?"

"I am." He placed her on the bed. "No one's ever understood me the way you did. No one ever listened to me that way, either. You didn't just listen -- you gave me the freedom to talk and be myself. I never thought that would be possible."

She smiled and kicked out of her shoes. "You're an amazing person."

"So are you." He dug in his pocket for the box. "I bought a ring. I want you to be more than my fated mate. I want you to be my wife, my partner, my lover."

"Eric." Her eyes misted with tears. "You're serious?"

"I am." He knelt before her and opened the box. "Will you be mine forever?"

She scooted to the edge of the bed. "I will." She held out her hand. "But you'd better make love to me. I've been thinking about being with you all day."

"I can't make you wait any longer." He slid the ring onto her finger. "Come here." He tugged her on top of him on the bed and kissed her. The second he did, his world righted. Everything that had been screwed up made sense. Everything wasn't fixed, but he had direction. He sucked on her tongue and touched her, caressing her ass, up her back and along her hips. He needed her nude. Now.

She pushed him to his back and straddled him. Within seconds, she whipped her blouse over her head. Her hair fluttered around her shoulders, and her breasts strained against the thin fabric of her bra. Her nipples beaded. A flush ran from her hairline to her chest.

He wished he hadn't worn a button-down shirt. Now that he was out of the service, he'd decided to dress up as little as possible. But it wasn't every day one met the queen. He wrestled out of his shirt, then shoved the garment out of sight. He slid his hands over her back again.

She grinned. "God, I love you."

"I love you, too." He'd never wanted anyone more. "My beautiful Valkyrie. I want you."

"You've got me." She unhooked her bra. The lingerie slipped loose, and she shoved it out of the way.

He groaned and buried his face in her cleavage before sucking on her nipple. She tasted like sin and sex. Intoxicating. He never wanted to be free from her spell.

She threaded her fingers into his hair. "Eric."

He wanted to hear her say his name forever. It sounded so sweet. She made his heart thunder and his blood thrum faster. He unzipped her jeans while continuing to suck on her nipples.

"Yes." She crawled off him long enough to shimmy out of her trousers. Before he realized what was happening, she stood nude before him.

He rushed to strip. He couldn't get naked fast enough. His cock throbbed, and he stroked himself. A shiver rocked through him. The raw desire to be one with her overwhelmed him. He'd never get enough. She was home -- his home. Anywhere he could be with her was perfect. "Come here."

"On that?" She crooked her brow, but her eyes sparkled. He loved the teasing tone of her voice. She inched up to him and crawled onto his lap again. "I like *that*." She kissed him as he grasped her hips.

Inch by inch, he filled her. He felt every ripple of

her pussy surrounding him. Christ, she was snug. Like she was made for him. He groaned.

"Yes." She rocked on him, grinding her hips. Her breasts jiggled with each movement. "More."

He loved the rosy tone of her breasts, the tiny points of her nipples, the flowery way she smelled and the fire in her eyes.

He bounced her, pushing her down to the hilt on his cock before nearly pulling out. Every push and rock nudged him closer to the edge. He wasn't going to be able to hold back for much longer.

Her hair fluttered again, and a fine sheen of perspiration glittered on her skin. She parted her lips. Her breath tickled his cheeks. Every squeeze of her body added to his pleasure. Like she held him within her. Needing him. Filling herself up with him and in turn, filling him up, too. She reassured him. Balanced him. Made him feel whole.

"More." She grasped his shoulders and moved faster. "Can't breathe. Love this."

He loved that he had her down to clipped sentences -- especially when he could barely think straight, much less talk. He sucked on her nipple. She moved up and down on his shaft.

Fuck. He truly wouldn't last. Not like this. He held onto her and rolled them onto the bed with her pinned beneath him. He pistoned into her, his desire overwhelming him. A feral need for her. He lost himself in the perfection of her body. She complemented him in life and made his heart beat. He'd never be the same. Why would he want to be?

"Eric." She crawled at his shoulders. "Faster. More."

He couldn't tell her no. Not right now. He braced himself on his knees and hands as he did as she asked.

He slammed into her, never wanting to part. Her cries of ecstasy turned him on. "Come with me," he said. He growled, and his actions turned disjointed.

She cried out again and tightened her legs around him. At the same time, she squeezed her pussy around his shaft. She tensed and shivered. Within a few seconds, she slumped beneath him. A lazy smile curled on her lips. "Come for me, too," she purred.

The dual movements added to his pleasure. So did her words. Hell, it all knocked him right over the edge. He embraced the climax as it rocked through him. The world seemed to slow to half speed, and his thoughts turned completely to mush. He added a couple more thrusts, then slowed. He stared at her. She was his girl. His Valkyrie. The woman of his heart. He was so fucking lucky.

He stilled above her and rested his forehead on hers. "Holy fuck."

"I second that. I love you, Eric." She tucked into him. "I can't imagine being anywhere else with the man of my heart."

"I love you, too."

"I can't wait for our life to continue to the next level," she said. "My mate."

He nodded. "Always my mate."

He held her and petted her hair. He'd found more than his heart when he'd run into her. He'd found a future and his soul. A chuckle bubbled in his throat. Coming to Eerie had been the best thing to happen to him.

Being taken by the Valkyrie had saved his life. Kara saved him. He never wanted to be free again. Ever.

Megan Slayer

Megan Slayer, aka Wendi Zwaduk, is a multi-published, award-winning author of more than one-hundred short stories and novels. She's been writing since 2008 and published since 2009. Her stories range from the contemporary and paranormal to LGBTQ and white-hot themes. No matter what the length, her works are always hot, but with a lot of heart. She enjoys giving her characters a second chance at love, no matter what the form. She's been nominated at the LRC for Best Author, Best Contemporary, Best Ménage, Best BDSM and Best Anthology. Her books have made it to the bestseller lists on various e-tailer sites.

When she's not writing, Megan spends time with her husband and son as well as three dogs and three cats. She enjoys art, music and racing, but football is her sport of choice. She's an active member of the Friends of the Keystone-LaGrange Public library.

Megan at Changeling: changelingpress.com/megan-slayer-a-161

Changeling Press LLC

Contemporary Action Adventure, Sci-Fi, Steampunk, Dark Fantasy, Urban Fantasy, Paranormal, and BDSM Romance available in e-book, audio, and print format at ChangelingPress.com – MC Romance, Werewolves, Vampires, Dragons, Shapeshifters and Horror -- Tales from the edge of your imagination.

Where can I get Changeling Press Books?

Changeling Press e-books are available at ChangelingPress.com, Amazon, Apple Books, Barnes & Noble, Kobo, Smashwords, and other online retailers, including Everand Subscription and Kobo Subscription Services. Print books are available at Amazon, Barnes and Noble, and by ISBN special order through your local bookstores.

Changeling Press, LLC

ChangelingPress.com